The

ROCKING CHAIR

The

ROCKING CHAIR

JOSHUA S. MAUNEY

TATE PUBLISHING & *Enterprises*

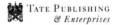

TATE PUBLISHING
& Enterprises

Tate Publishing is committed to excellence in the publishing industry. Our staff of highly trained professionals, including editors, graphic designers, and marketing personnel, work together to produce the very finest books available. The company reflects the philosophy established by the founders, based on Psalms 68:11,

"THE LORD GAVE THE WORD AND GREAT WAS THE COMPANY OF THOSE WHO PUBLISHED IT."

If you would like further information, please contact us:
1.888.361.9473 | www.tatepublishing.com
TATE PUBLISHING & Enterprises, LLC | 127 E. Trade Center Terrace
Mustang, Oklahoma 73064 USA

Published in the United States of America

ISBN:978-1-6024712-2-1

07.02.26

DEDICATION

To the Atwell Family, thank you for the inspiration.

To my Dad, thank you for teaching me about love
and second chances.

Kristen, thank you for believing

ONE

As she sat on the back porch over looking the lake, Kristen Taylor could do little more than rock back and forth and stare at the second hand on her watch. As the seconds turned into minutes and the minutes turned into an hour, her rocking became more nervous and her glimpses at the watch became more frequent. Kristen was a natural beauty with dark brown hair, tan skin, and eyes that were so blue they almost seemed to glow against her complexion. Today, however, those eyes were filled with a kind of nervous anxiety that she had never felt before. Her eyes stayed fixed out on the lake scanning back and forth as if searching for something from a long time ago.

The day had started out like any other day, and upon waking up that morning she had no reason to believe that this day would be any different. Home from college, the twenty-two-year-old was enjoying some much needed rest and recovery time, and it was a nice feeling to just be home for a little while. Home was a little town called Cartersville tucked quietly up in the northeast corner of Georgia. It was a perfect southern town where people still waved as they drove by and where high school football on Friday night was king. It was a Saturday morning in early summer and the day had turned into a day that most southerners dream about. It was not too hot and not too cold and the sun shown down on all of the green that had begun to blossom. The lake was busy with people fishing and riding their boats with a couple of skiers now and then who were too impatient to let the lake water warm up. Kristen had gotten up late that morning and as the sun came sneaking through the curtains and the birds began their usual song, it seemed as if the day was trying to call her out of bed. Clad in a pair of light tan shorts and a light blue tank top, and glad to be out of the winter clothes for a while, she stumbled her way downstairs and into the large open kitchen to get something to eat.

She felt a great sense of peace there in her parent's home. Scanning around the kitchen and out into the living room, memories of the years she had spent there came working their way back to her. She had spent many happy days there at the house on the lake, and even though she was still groggy from sleep, she wore a smile on her face as she shuffled around the kitchen.

Throwing some butter on a piece of bread and trying to shake the sleep out of her brain, she spotted a list on the counter that had been carefully placed on the edge so that it would not get lost in all of the clutter. It was a list of things for her to do that day that her father had left for her. This was the usual routine around her house, and it seemed to make little difference to her father that she was only home for the summer.

Every morning she would go downstairs to find her family already out and about for the day with a list left behind of things she needed to do if she ever made it out of bed. The rest of the day was usually filled with one reason or another of why none of it could be done which always gave way to the frustrated look on her Dad's face that night.

This morning she was going to do her best to get some of it done, if for no other reason than to avoid the conversation with her Dad that she knew would come when he discovered she had exchanged raking for boat rides and cleaning with a nap down on the dock. Scanning the list for the easiest task she found near the bottom of the list in a hieroglyphic style pen *wash your car.* Figuring this would be the most painless of all of the jobs she chocked down the last bite of buttered bread and made her way out into the garage to scrape together a bucket, soap, and rags.

With the stereo turned up all the way she sprayed down the dirt and pollen covered jeep and began giving it a much needed cleaning. With the radio booming, the sun beaming down, and the light cool feeling in the air, the dread of the manual labor had been replaced with content as she worked her way around the jeep. She had been cleaning for about and hour and was just putting the finishing touches on her car when she heard her phone ring. She tried to dry her hands and get to the phone but she was a second too late. She thought it better to finish up the car and let whoever it was leave a message. Turning back up the radio and returning the phone to the hood of her car, she paid little thought to the voicemail message blinking on her phone. She began cleaning out the inside of her jeep that looked more like a clothes hamper and less like the inside of a car. The jeep was full of clothes and CDs strewn everywhere, a half eaten bag of chips in the seat and countless other odds and ends.

With her car in its current condition, her mind was on more important things than phone calls. She cleaned out the inside of her car and hummed along with the radio as her mind wandered to thoughts of next year. She was approaching her senior year of college and it was getting close to time to decide what it was she was going to do and where it was she was going to go. Like most people in her position, there was a certain degree of excitement about going out into the world but it was covered with a healthy amount of fear about what to expect. She was a smart girl, and her father, a doctor in town, had been after her pretty hard lately to try and get motivated with her school work. Even though she was very smart, the one lazy bone that she did have in her body seemed to be directly connected to the left hand that was supposed to be doing her work. She could just hear her dad right now, "There is nothing worse than great potential." It was the sarcastic quip that he always threw at her when she couldn't find the motivation to do her work. She thought about him saying it as she rolled her eyes as if she thought he might be able to see it and then continued piling up the trash bag full of dirty clothes that she had rescued from the jeep.

She closed the doors to her jeep and carried the stack of clothes into the house before she remembered the phone that she had placed on the hood of her car. She made a quick trip back outside and as she grabbed the phone she could see the voicemail light still blinking red. She went in through the garage door and back into the kitchen flipping the phone open to check the number and hear the message. She didn't recognize the number at all. She figured that the out of state area code was probably a wrong number but she pressed send on the phone to check the message. She flipped open the cabinet door to grab a cup, and as she proceeded through the list of commands to get to the message, she reached into the fridge to get some ice for her glass of water. With her glass in one hand and the phone pinned between her ear and her shoulder, she picked up a hand full of ice to drop into the glass. Before the ice could make it into the glass she heard a voice on the phone that made her freeze in place and she took a deep breath as she felt the chills run down her back.

Hey baby girl, it's me. It's been a long time. I am hoping that you are in town this weekend. I got your number from my aunt. I hope you don't mind. I am back now. I just moved into a house close to where I grew up. I was hoping if you aren't busy tonight that maybe I could come see you. I think you have something of mine and I was hoping I could come back and get it. I know you probably have a lot going on and lot of people to get caught up with so if you are too busy I understand. The number that I called you from is my new phone, so if you want too just call me back on that number. I hope I will talk to you later. Bye.

TWO

She stood there in the kitchen in disbelief as if she were afraid to move. She thought that maybe if she moved the dream that she had just had would go away. The ice that she had in her hand had still not made it to the cup and as she stood there the look on her face seemed as frozen as her hand. She put the cup and the ice down slowly, afraid she would somehow hit a wrong button and erase the message. She found herself sitting in the middle of the kitchen on the floor trying to blow some warm air on her frozen hand. *I can't believe that he called.* She sat there for a few minutes to collect her thoughts and then hit the button on the phone to listen to the message one more time. As the message played through a second time, her mind began to race back to a summer when she was a young girl and the flood of emotions was almost more than she could stand. It took listening to the message three more times before she had finally begun to believe that it was real. Almost as quickly as she realized that the call was real, she realized that she would have to call him back.

The voice on the phone was Jackson Bryce, and it was one she had not heard in about four years. She was only a girl when he lived there in town, but she could remember every second as if it were yesterday. More than the memories, she could remember every second that he had been gone. They hadn't spoken since the day he left. Last she heard, he had moved to a town up in North Carolina and was doing some kind of work up there. She had tried to look him up a couple of times but it was obvious that he was not trying to be found. She had spent many sleepless nights wondering if he would ever come back.

For any person that has ever felt love it always feels the same. It is that first time that a person feels like they can't make it another second without the other person being there and the first time they feel like they might die because the other person is in the room. It's the first time that they become the loudest person in a crowded room so that they will be noticed and silent as a mouse when it's just the two of them alone because they don't know what to say. For Kristen it was no different, and as she thought back on her time with Jackson a nervous feeling crept over her body that she had not felt in a long time. She reached nervously for the phone as she stood up from her place on the floor. She stared at the number trying to find the nerve to press the send button.

Too nervous to stay in one place, she paced back and forth through the kitchen and back out into the living room and then back again. She was trying to think of what to say but the words weren't sounding right in her head. *Hey Jackson, how's it going?* No, that sounds too casual she thought. *Good afternoon, Jackson, how have you been lately?* No, no, no that sounds like I am interviewing him for a job. *What's up Jack?* No, she didn't think that would be good either. She had picked the phone up a couple of times to hit send but she was trying to find a way to pull herself together. She didn't want to seem jittery or nervous. She didn't want to let on how much this phone call meant to her.

Still dazed from the flood of emotions, she was back on the floor again trying to pull her thoughts together, and after a few minutes she was able to get up to walk into the bathroom to take a look at the mirror. *Gah! I look rough.* She began teasing her hair that had gotten damp from washing the car and tried to straighten out her shirt as she hit send on the telephone still fixing and primping as if he would somehow be able to see her. She had not talked to Jackson in about four years, but it had only been a few months since she had finally quit thinking about him. The phone rang two, three, then four times, and just as she was preparing to come up with a message to leave, a familiar voice answered back on the other end.

"Hello?"

"Jackson?" Kristen asked, even though she already knew it was him.

"Yeah. Kristen is that you? Wow. I was hoping you would call me back."

His voice sounded the same to her but to Jackson she didn't sound the same at all. The voice that he used to talk to everyday had been replaced with a woman's voice and it caught him off guard for just a second.

"So, you are back in town now?" Kristen asked. She was trying her best to stay calm and to sound collected on the phone. Her hand was shaking as she held the phone to her ear, and as she stared into the bathroom mirror she could see the smile that beamed across her face. "Your message said that you have a house."

"Yeah, I am here. It took me a little longer than I had planned but I am back. I guess I have been here for about a week or so. I was kind of hoping that we could get together. It's been forever. I can't believe it has been four years. How is your family? What's your dad doing? I bet your sister has gotten big. What's your mom been up to?"

"Hah," Kristen laughed, not sure which question to answer first. "Well Dad is doing good, still working all the time. You know him never slows down for anything. Mom is good. She is still doing the same old thing, and Alyson has grown a bunch since you saw her last. I bet you wouldn't even recognize her, she is ten now and still meaner than ever."

They both laughed for a second and then the phone went silent. It had been years since they had shared a laugh, and more than being a happy reminder of the time they had spent together, it quickly became a reminder of how long it had been. Almost instantly the mood was somber and the seconds ticked by without either one of them knowing what to say.

"Well, I was hoping I could see you tonight if you aren't busy," Jackson said with an almost hesitant tone.

All Kristen could manage to say was, "Well I will be at the house this evening if you want to come by. You know where it is." Her mind was racing because all she wanted to do was yell or cry. She wanted to ask him where he had been. Why had it been so long since he had called or written, but the words just wouldn't come out.

"Is five o'clock ok?" Jackson asked.

"Yeah that sounds great. I will see you then." Kristen replied.

"Ok, see you in a little while. Bye."

As he said goodbye, Kristen hung up the phone. *Goodbye.* It was the saddest word in the entire world she thought. She remembered the last time he had said it to her and after a couple of years of waiting with no response, she had come to believe that it would be the last time that he would ever say it to her. She still couldn't believe that he was back in town and after all this time she wondered what he would think of her. Looking at her watch she realized that she only had an hour to get ready before he would be there. She also knew that he was not one to be late. She ran up to her room to take a shower and even though the phone call was bittersweet in a way, she could not help the feeling of excitement that was beginning to creep over her.

On the other side of town Jackson Bryce placed his cell phone back into his pocket and smiled from ear to ear. It had been a long time since he had talked to her, and even though he had done his best to sound calm, the lump in his throat told a different story. After a few minutes, his nerves began to settle again and his breathing was back under control. He had not thought that it was going to be that difficult to talk to her. He reached into the bottom drawer of the desk where he was sitting and pulled out a few sheets of paper and a pen. He felt kind of juvenile having to write down everything that he wanted to say but he knew that he would never get the words to come out right. It took about forty-five minutes to write his letter and looking at the clock he knew that he better get going. He took great care to fold the letter and placed the pages into an envelope. On the outside of the envelope was simply a large K. He sealed it shut, and realizing that if he didn't hurry he would be late ran out to his car and sped down the driveway.

Kristen had started the water for the shower and as she undressed to climb in, she took a look into the mirror. Turning to the side and then back to the front she looked at her body. It had changed quite a lot over the last few years and she wondered what Jackson would think when he saw her. She had a beautiful body with tan legs that gave way to ample curves all resting on a long slender torso. As she pulled back her hair it revealed her long slender neck that seemed to provide her athletic frame with a sense of elegance. Hanging around her neck was an old faded necklace that she never took off. The old beat up looking necklace looked out of place on such a beautiful body but she had been wearing it so long that most of the time she forgot it was even there. From time to time she would feel it there under her shirt and no matter what kind of mood she was in it always made her smile.

The water had gotten warm and so she slid into the shower almost slipping as she made it into the tub. Her nerves and excitement were getting the best of her, and as she let the water run down her back, she tried to let what had just happened sink in a little bit. The steam rose up in the bathroom from the hot shower. She tried desperately to regain some composure. She did not want to appear like an excited little girl when he got there so she took several deep breathes to try and steady her nerves.

She toweled off quickly and threw the towel around herself as she slide in front of the mirror to dry her hair. Even though she and Jackson had spent an entire summer together it still felt almost like a first date as she pulled out the hair dryer to fix her long brown hair. Looking in the mirror to fix her hair, her eyes quickly traveled down to her mouth which was beaming with a smile that she had not smiled in a long time. She tried to put it away but the more she thought the bigger the smile became. After drying her hair, she headed into her bedroom to find something to wear. The pile of clothes that had been in her car now lay thrown on the floor next to several piles of clothes that had found themselves on the floor many days before. Throwing open the closet doors, she rummaged through what clean clothes she had and found a pair of jeans and a shirt to throw on. She trotted back into the bathroom to check out her outfit in the mirror and after a quick inspection found herself back in the closet looking for another shirt.

The clock on the night stand read four forty-five and she knew it wouldn't be long until he got there. She could feel herself tensing up, but after four shirts and two pairs of jeans she knew she had found the right combination. She slid back in front of the bathroom mirror for one last inspection before giving herself an approving nod. She headed downstairs to the living room to wait on him to get there. The house was deathly quiet. Her mom and sister had gone out for the day and her dad was at work and so she was the only person left alone in the house. She quickly realized that the silence was deafening. She went to the radio to turn on some music. The CD in the player was an instrumental tape and she laughed when she heard it. *He's gonna think he walked into an elevator.* She dug through her CD case and threw in some classic rock and hit play, and as Led Zeppelin began to drift out through the house she went and found a seat on the couch.

She threw her hair back and cocked her leg up on the couch trying to look casual and hoping to not appear too excited when he got there. She was chewing on one of her fingernails and tapping her foot furiously on the ground. After only a minute on the couch, she moved over to the large chair that sat over in the corner of the room. She shifted from side to side trying to get comfortable but her nerves wouldn't let her sit still. *I am gonna look creepy sitting over here in this dark corner.* Looking at her watch she knew that he would probably be there any second, so she decided to go sit out on the back porch over-looking the lake. She spotted the large white rocking chair resting on one end of the porch and she moved over to it to take a seat. She found comfort in the rocking chair on the porch and she felt the tension begin to dissipate as she rocked back and forth. The sun still had a couple of hours left up in the sky and the air had become that cool crisp feeling that can only truly be appreciated in the south. Her watch read five o'clock and as she sat there rocking she couldn't help but think back. Her rocking became more nervous and the second hand made another trip around her watch as her mind began to drift back to four summers ago when she met him for the first time.

THREE

The first time she ever met Jackson she had just turned eighteen years old, and even though almost five years had passed since then, she could remember it like it was yesterday. Kristen's dad was a doctor there in town, and had volunteered to do free physicals for the football team at the local high school. Dr. Taylor was not a big guy and even though he had never been much of a football player, he was the kind of guy that enjoyed it all. He had the build of a runner and his small frame was topped off with surprisingly broad shoulders. The fifty-year-old man's hair was gray where he had any left at all, and never wanting to get too old to do anything, he was still in great shape. His hands were very nimble as if every movement was some type of surgical procedure, and as he examined teenager after teenager a look of boredom was beginning to creep over his face. It was beautiful outside and the May weather had not yet completely given way to the tortuous hot summer months and he longed to be outside to enjoy some of it. Quick witted and the constant joker, he had tried to make idle conversation with the athletes as they shuffled through the line but he quickly realized he was playing to an impossible crowd.

Sitting one of the players up on the examining table, he was beginning the usual blood pressure and heart rate checks, and running down the list of questions that he had to ask every player.

"Do you have any injuries or pain that you would like me to look at?" he asked as he wrapped the stethoscope around his neck.

The offensive lineman that they just called Mantooth stared back at the doctor with no response. He was a large kid and the examination table groaned and creaked when he shifted back and forth pondering the question. Even sitting down on the table he was still at eye level with the doctor. His expression looked blank. It didn't look like he was ignoring the doctor but more like the question was simply taking a few minutes to process. It appeared as if he was temporarily shutting down to let his brain focus on the question.

Jokingly, Dr. Taylor made an imaginary check next to head trauma and trying to keep from laughing said, "So, buddy, any head injuries?"

The confused football player had finally caught up with the conversation and in a deep throaty voice replied with an abrupt, "No."

"You sure?" the doctor asked half jokingly and half wondering just how many times this kid had taken a shot to the head.

The questioning had become too much for Mantooth and he said, "We done, I need to go to the weight room."

"Yeah were done," the doctor answered. *You might want to take a trip down to study hall if you have a minute* he thought as he signed his name to the bottom of the physical form. The giant lineman slid off the table and planted his size fourteen feet down onto the floor. When he stretched out his frame he looked as if he might be able to pick the doctor up and put him in his pocket.

"Alright buddy, you can go." With that the lineman made a quick turn on his heel and headed out of the locker room door pointed straight for the weight room.

Dr. Taylor had been dealing with the knuckle draggers all day, so when his next patient came sliding up onto his table, he was relieved to have someone that looked like they might be able to make some conversation.

Looking at the physical form, he read the name at the top of the page. He half mumbled to himself, "Jackson Bryce."

"Yes sir," the young man replied. "Everybody just calls me Jack."

"Ok Jack," Doctor Taylor replied, "You have anything you want me to check out? You got anything hurting or giving you problems?" He flipped through the form to see if anything jumped out at him.

"Well I think I was stung by something, Doc," Jackson replied. As he said it, he rolled up his sleeve to reveal the flexed bicep that he had curled up in a body builder pose. "I think that I am getting some swelling."

The doctor laughed, thankful to have someone do something besides sit on the table and turn their head and cough. "Yeah, I see that," he said, "But don't worry the swelling looks pretty minimal, should be gone by the morning." They both laughed and as he continued with the examination the two continued chatting as if they were old friends. The longer that they talked, the more the doctor became impressed with the young man.

Jackson was eighteen years old but his dark green eyes looked much older. It was obvious to the doctor and to anyone that knew him that he was carrying around much more than the normal burdens of a teenager. His eyes spoke of a quiet sadness that he kept hidden behind a square jaw that supported the massive smile that he flashed from time to time. This all rested on a frame that was surprisingly muscular for his age and with his shirt pulled off, the muscles on his chest and arms writhed under his skin each time he moved. The bold farmer's tan told the tale of many hours of working outside in the hot Georgia sun.

The examination was nothing spectacular and it was obvious to Dr. Taylor that the kid was in great shape. The physical seemed more of a formality than a real physical.

"So what year are you, Jack," the doctor asked.

"Well, um I actually just graduated sir," Jackson replied.

"Oh, well what are you doing here? These are physicals for the football players." The doctor said with a look of confusion on his face.

Jackson lowered his voice and leaned towards the doctor, "Well I really don't have much money, sir, so the closest thing I figured I could get to a doctor's appointment was to come by here. Is that wrong? I mean I didn't mean to waste your time."

"Oh no," Dr. Taylor replied. "Doesn't matter to me son, I have already looked at fifty kids today one more wouldn't hurt anything. I won't tell," he said flashing a quick wink at Jackson before proceeding through the examination.

Jackson smiled, relieved that the doctor was being so nice, and he hoped that none of the guys in the line behind him had heard what he had said.

"So any plans for next year? Have you given any thought to college?" The doctor asked.

"Oh, yes sir, I have, I think about it most everyday. I just don't think I will have enough money to go to school right out so I was thinking about going into the military. I hear that they will give you money for school as long as you go in for a couple of years. I don't know," he said with a pause. "I kind of need to stay close to help watch out for my little brothers. So I am not sure what I am gonna do just yet."

The doctor's mind flashed back to almost thirty years ago, and he could remember being in the same spot. It was only after a few years in the navy that he was able to have enough money to go to school and then on to medical school. Dr. Taylor knew about having to work for what he wanted and he could see that same spark in Jackson. Flashing a knowing smile at Jackson he said, "Well yeah buddy, that's right they will help pay for your school. Just what

ever you do, don't be a Marine. I hear they make you walk a lot."
They both laughed.

Looking at the physical form that he had in his hand, the doctor was writing his last couple of notes on the page.

"You can go ahead and put your shirt back on," the doctor said. "Wouldn't want any more insect bites on those little arms, at least till the other swelling goes down."

Jackson laughed as he slid back on the old t-shirt that was obviously a hand me down from someone and hopped down off the table. He quickly reached up to fix his neatly cut brown hair, and did his best to get straightened up before heading out of the door.

"Well thanks a bunch, Doc, I guess I will see you around," as he said it he stuck his hand out to the doctor. Dr. Taylor was caught off guard by the gesture for a second and was even more surprised at the strength in the young man's grip. They shook hands for a second and as Jackson turned to leave the doctor grabbed back at his hand.

"Hey buddy, how would you like to make a little money this summer?"

Jackson looked confused for a minute and his face definitely showed that he didn't quite understand the proposition.

"Well I don't think I am ready to do any surgeries just yet, Doc. We have only dissected frogs in biology so far," he replied in a half joking half confused way.

Dr. Taylor laughed, "No, I have some work I need help getting done around the house and I was thinking you might be able to do it. It's nothing too major, but I just don't have time and you look like the kind of fella that might be able to get it done."

"Ok, yeah, I could that for you," Jackson replied.

"Well here is my number, call me next week and we will see what we can work out." As he said it Dr. Taylor slide a business card into the young man's hand.

"Ok, cool, thanks a lot, Dr. Taylor, I sure will. Well, I better get going I have to go pick up my little brothers and take them home, but I will call you."

"Ok Jack, see you buddy. Oh and call me Ed."

"Ok thanks, Ed," Jackson shot back. With that, Jackson did a quick about face and headed toward the door, sliding the card down into the back pocket of his wrangler blue jeans.

Kristen smiled as she rocked back and forth in the chair thinking about that day. She figured that she had probably heard the story about a hundred times from her father. The conversation had come up several times over the years and it was one of her Dad's many stories that she never got tired of hearing. She was still sitting on the rocking chair on the back porch and as she looked at her watch it read five fifteen. It was not like Jackson to be late. She was growing more and more anxious wondering what could be keeping him, and as the rhythm of the rocking chair settled into a beat of creaks and groans from the wood, her mind started to drift off again.

FOUR

Jackson Bryce had made it to the end of the street in his small black sports car and took a hard right up Cassville road towards the highway. He had thought about Kristen every single day for the last four years but he had not been prepared for the way that he would feel when he heard her voice on the other end of the line. He looked at the clock on the dash in time to realize that he was running way behind. The time he had taken to write the letter that lay on the seat next to him had set him back more than he had expected. He hated being late for anything, but he had to write the letter. He knew that once he saw her he would never be able to say all of the things he needed to say. He punched on the gas as he flew past Cass Grocery and the old fire department. As he came past the old high school his mind drifted back to the summer where it all started.

Jackson kept his word and he called Dr. Taylor early that next Monday morning. It was the end of May and the Georgia sun was already beating down at eight in the morning when he pulled up in the driveway of the lakefront home. The air was thick and the dew was beginning to burn off of the grass and it was hard to even move around outside without feeling sticky and gross. Jackson parked at the top of the steep downhill driveway, and as the door squeaked shut on his old pickup truck, he stood in awe of the massive house. He had gotten directions from Ed that morning and he could only guess if he had come to the right house. The house was massive, much larger than the three bedroom home that Jackson lived in with his family and he couldn't help feeling out of place as he looked at his old beat up truck and his old faded Levis.

Nervously, he made his way to the door still surveying the area and hoping that he had come to the right house. He made it to the front door and just as he was reaching for the doorbell, the front door swung open and Ed emerged from inside of the massive entry way. He looked different then he did the day that Jackson saw him for the physical. He was wearing a Hawaiian shirt half unbuttoned and a pair of running shorts. He was working on his third cup of coffee and the rich smell from the cup caught Jackson's nose. The smell reminded him of his father, and at that moment he missed him a lot.

"Well, hey buddy, you made it," Ed said. "Come on in the house here and let me finish this cup of coffee and I will show you around."

"Ok Doc," Jackson said.

They headed in through the front door; and Jackson couldn't help but stumble through in awe. The large twenty foot ceilings and enormous stone fireplace made Jackson feel as if he had walked into another world. The house was decorated like a cabin with large outdoor style paintings on the walls, and earth toned furniture that managed to provide the giant house with a homey feel. They rounded the corner of the large spiral stair case that wound its way upstairs to several rooms. They turned the corner and were in the kitchen. The entire rear of the house was a series of windows that gave a perfect view of the lake from every angle. The kitchen, dining room, and living room were all connected into one enormous space that made Jackson feel very small. They settled into some chairs in the kitchen where Ed had been reading the paper and going over some notes from the hospital.

"You find the place ok?" Ed asked.

"Yes Sir, came right to it; you gave good directions."

"Well of course," Ed popped back with a smile. Ed was horrible at giving directions. He assumed that whoever he was giving the instructions to knew half of the turns already, so he was notorious for just giving people the "general gist" of where they needed to go.

"You want a cup of coffee, buddy?" Ed asked.

"Oh no sir, I think I have already had a pot this morning," Jackson replied. They sat there in silence for a minute as Ed finished reading the last section of the paper. Jackson kept looking around trying to keep from gawking at the larger than life house.

Almost all at once, as if reading the current events had just given him a jolt of life, Ed sprung up from the table and said, "Come on, buddy, lets show you around the place."

They went through the house where Ed pointed out all of the various rooms. The house seemed like some kind of museum to Jackson. You could have easily fit his entire house in the kitchen and following Ed from room to room made him feel lost and out of place. They traveled up the large curved staircase and towards the bedrooms.

"Those are my girl's rooms," Ed said as he pointed to the end of the hallway. "I have two girls, Kristen and Alyson, but they are asleep. Unless you swing through here around lunchtime, you probably won't see much of them. My oldest, Kristen, just graduated too. Do you guys know each other?"

Jackson hesitated before he answered. He was temporarily lost in his own thoughts.

"No sir, we went to different schools, so we never met," he finally replied.

He couldn't help but be a little jealous at the thought of sleeping in late one morning. They spun back around to point out the master bedroom before quickly moving back down the stairs and into the basement where he showed Jackson the small gym that he had set up down there. The house seemed to go on and on and to Jackson, who shared a room with both of his brothers, it seemed like some kind of paradise. Without wasting much time, they were back upstairs and out into the garage where Jackson was given a brief overview of all of the tools and toys that he could find out there. To Jackson, it looked like a place where trinkets went to die. There was stuff piled up in the corners ranging from Christmas ornaments to ski boots, and everything in between. Most of the things in that garage had not been used much since the day they were brought to the house and had only been taken into the garage to make room for more things to go inside.

"Ok buddy, any kind of tools you need will be in here," Ed said. "Good luck finding them. Let's go down to the dock and I will show you what I want to have you do."

They rounded the corner of the driveway and down a rock pathway that led to a large dock that floated in their inlet of the lake. Tied to the dock rested a large pontoon boat, a ski boat, and a pair of jet skis. Jackson had never seen anything like it and he tried to act casual as he looked at all of the toys laid out in the water. The dock was very large and had an upper and lower level. The railing around the sides looked busted up and there were boards that needed to be fixed. The winter storms had taken their toll. The upper level was accessible through an unfinished staircase of loose boards, and the wear was obvious.

"You ever do any skiing, buddy?"

"Um, no sir, I haven't." Jackson replied. *Heck I've never even been on a boat like that before.*

"Well then we will just have to teach you," Ed said with a smile. When he said it, his bright blue eyes lit up as if the thought of getting to teach Jackson to ski made him happier than skiing himself.

"This is what I want you to do," as he said it he pointed at the half formed set of stairs that went up to the top of the dock. He had obviously been working on it before but he just hadn't had time to finish the project. "I want you to finish the steps first," he said. "I have already done all of the cutting and everything has been made. All I need you to do it screw all of the boards down and make sure everything is sanded real good so nobody gets any splinters. You think you can handle it?"

"Oh yes sir," Jackson shot back. He had done work like this around the house before and even though he wasn't that good at it, he always found a way to make it work. Jackson's parents weren't together and he never really knew his dad. He had been given the role of man of the house years before a boy should have to worry about such things. The weight of all that he had been through seemed almost more than his broad shoulders could handle. He had had to step up around the house and be a sort of father figure to his two brothers and sister. He also knew that every dime that he made that summer would have to go to his mother to help her out any way he could.

"Well buddy, I guess that should be enough to get you started. It should probably take you a couple of hours to get everything finished up. I have to run up to the office and take care of some stuff but just make yourself at home."

"Yes sir, I will."

"If you have any questions or you need to get up with me or you can't find the tools you need, just run up to the house and ask Kristen or Alyson. You've met my daughters haven't you?"

"Um, no sir, I haven't, but if I can't find what I am looking for I will find them."

"Ok buddy, I am heading out. Be careful, and call me if you need anything."

"Ok thanks, Dr. Taylor, uh I mean Ed. I will."

With that, Ed went bounding up the stairs and out to his car. Jackson couldn't help but be impressed at how athletic the doctor was and wondered if he would still be in such good shape when he was fifty. As he turned back to the project at hand, he made a quick survey of all the tools that he would need. It was a long way from the house to the dock up and down a hill and he wanted to make as few trips as possible.

Walking back up to the top of the hill, he couldn't help but be impressed at everything that was around him. The cars, the boats, the giant house, all seemed like something he had seen on *Lifestyles of the Rich and Famous* and he kept having to remind himself to not just stand around with his mouth open. He had managed to come up with almost everything that he needed and he moved back down to the dock to start working.

It was about nine thirty in the morning and the sun was beginning to get up in the sky. Carefully laying out the boards and checking to see if everything would fit, he started at the bottom step and began working on fastening the board to the brackets. Jackson was a strong young man and he got great use out of every turn of his screwdriver. Each time he would make a turn, the muscles on his arms would tense and flex and the stern look on his face looked more like the face of a surgeon at work than a kid fastening boards to a dock.

After finally getting the first few boards on, Jackson looked through his assortment of tools and hardware to find the other screws. He had thought that he would have enough but he had forgotten that it was going to take four per board instead of two, and so he was going to run out before the job was finished. He laid down his tools and began the hike back up the hill towards the garage. His arms were tight from the work and sweat had begun to run down his arms and chest, as it soaked through his t-shirt.

Digging through the mess in the garage was taking forever and he still had not managed to find the screws that he needed to finish the job. Not wanting to bother the girls but more so not wanting to waste any more time, he headed toward the door. He walked to the door of the garage that led back into the house and gave it a loud knock as he turned the handle to go inside.

"Hello? Anybody in here?"

No one answered but he saw a head poke out from behind the couch. He walked over and found the spy tucked in behind the pillows that normally covered the couch.

"Kristen?" He asked not sure which one of the daughters he was talking to.

"No! Kristen is outside," the voice said from behind the pillows. Never lifting her head from behind the pillows she pointed a finger out to the back porch that had a view of the dock where he had been talking with Ed. Jackson could barely hear the little girl from under the stack of pillows but following the tiny finger out to the back porch he could see a girl in the rocking chair with her back to the door.

"Kristen?" he asked, as he walked out onto the back porch. "The pillows told me you would be out here."

"What?" She said as she turned around to face him, not really getting the joke.

"You're Kristen, right?" he asked.

"Yeah, that was Alyson; she is scared of boys," she said as she rose from the chair.

As Kristen turned around to greet the stranger, she was taken aback. She had much more enjoyed the conversation before she turned around. Almost immediately, her face turned red, and she hoped that he could not tell. She had known that her father was going to have someone out at the house working, but she never imagined that they would look like Jackson Bryce. His face had a dark tan and sweat dripped down from his hair and face. His shirt was soaked with sweat and his arms seemed massive to her. When their eyes met, neither one of them really knew what to say, and so for what seemed like an hour they both just stared.

Jackson was having a tough time catching his breath as he watched Kristen rise from her chair. Wearing only a pair of shorts and a tank top, her clothes did nothing to hide her figure and he was looking for something to say that might break the silence.

"Jack . . . um . . . me . . . I mean I'm Jackson. Hi, I'm Jackson, but my friends just call me Jack," he said, stumbling over each word.

"Hi, I'm Kristen," she said. She could feel how red her cheeks must be and thought that they must look like they were on fire to him.

Trying to keep down the awkward silence, Jackson said, "Well listen, I was looking for a box of screws and your dad told me that if I needed help finding something to come find you. You got any idea where I could find them?"

"Um . . . I don't know but I will go look." *Gee thanks for letting me know Dad!*

"So you like it up here?" Jackson asked trying to make conversation.

"Yeah it's fine," Kristen replied, not really wanting to get in too much small talk. She had known that there was going to be someone out at the house to do some work but she never imagined a young man like Jackson. If she would have known that Jackson was going to be there she would have been sure to lock herself in her room.

They both headed out into the garage to search for the screws and in the time it took them to find the screws, it had started to get pretty hot outside.

"Well I sure do think this is a beautiful place out here. Must be pretty cool living on the lake," Jackson said, still trying to fill the silence with something.

"Yeah it's fine," Kristen replied. She wished so badly that she had known he was coming so that she could have put something else on, or at least taken a shower.

Jackson couldn't tell if it was the heat that had him so flustered or if it was Kristen there next to him, and after rummaging through the piles of stuff he was kind of disappointed when Kristen turned to hand him the box of screws. He took the box from her and managed to get out a quick thank you before she headed for the door to the house. The door closed behind her and Jackson headed back towards the dock. He did his best to pull himself together. He was sure that she was the most beautiful girl that he had ever seen and as he headed back down to the dock to finish his work for the day his mind was racing. He did his best to keep his mind on his work, but between the heat and seeing Kristen he wasn't sure how to focus.

The sun was beating down hard and Jackson had started to work up a pretty good sweat. With no shade out on the dock, the water was beginning to look more and more inviting. He had been back to work for about an hour when he heard some footsteps tiptoeing out onto the dock. He looked up to see Kristen easing out on to the dock almost as if she had not wanted to be seen. As he finished tightening one more screw, she reached out a large glass of ice water.

"Here you go," she said.

Before he could even mutter a thank you, she turned and sprinted back up the stairs and back towards the house. The ice water was nice and he thought little of her not wanting to be out there in the heat. He was kind of glad she had left as quickly as she did because he was not sure what he would have said. She was breath taking and as he watched her make it to the top of the hill, he had to shake himself to get his mind back on the job he was doing.

He had been working for several hours and was putting the finishing touches on the steps as the sun began to ease down on the far side of the lake. The breeze that began to blow across the water was the kind of cool that can only be enjoyed after a long day of work in the sun. His shirt was wet with sweat and he was just picking up the last of his tools when he heard Ed call out to him.

"How's it coming along, buddy?" Ed yelled as he made his way to the dock.

"Good sir, bout got it finished. I was just picking up the tools and was gonna head home."

"Head home?" Ed shot back surprised. "I was hoping we could take a ride on the boat."

"Oh. I would love to, Ed, but I need to get back and square up some dinner for my brothers. Could we go another time?"

"Yeah buddy, that would be fine." Ed couldn't help but be impressed at the young man. He didn't know what Jackson's situation was at home but he could tell that he was carrying a heavy load. The teenager's eyes told it all. "Well let's see what you've got done today." He examined the work with the eye of a military drill instructor. Jackson held his breath not wanting to disappoint. Ed looked around the steps and smiled his half smile and simply said, "Well you got it done at least." It was Ed's way of saying good job without having to actually come out and say it, but Jackson didn't know that and he took the backhanded compliment to mean that Ed wasn't satisfied.

"Well do you have anything you want me to do tomorrow?" Jackson asked half expecting a quick, no, followed by a, don't call us we'll call you.

Ed simply said, "Yeah I think I have some stuff for you. Can you be back at seven in the morning?"

"Yeah sir, seven it is." With that they gathered up the last of the tools and headed towards the house. Walking back up the hill with the Doctor filled Jackson with a kind of peace that he had not felt in a long time. Not having a father around he had missed these little moments and so when Ed patted him on the back as they made it to the top of the hill, he felt a lump form in his throat. He had not realized how lonely he felt until he stood there at the bottom the driveway. His head was reeling from the hard days work. The two of them stood there for a moment, both enjoying the moment of quiet, when Jackson glanced down at his watch.

"Well, Doc, I better get on the road," he said, not really wanting to leave. He was scared that if he ever left this paradise he had found he might not ever find his way back.

"Well, I hate you have to go," Ed said. "But maybe next time we can try strapping on some skis and giving it a run."

"Yeah, I would like that," Jackson replied. He stuck out his hand and the Doctor met it with his. They shook quickly before Jackson turned towards his truck. Ed watched him to the top of the hill before turning to go inside. As he walked back into the garage, he reached for the screwdriver that Jackson had laid on the tool bench. Smiling to himself and keeping back so he wouldn't be seen, Ed waited patiently in the garage until Jackson was gone so that he could go back down and fix the steps that had not been screwed on just right.

Jackson made it to the top of the hill and back up to his truck. He was bone tired from his day out on the dock. He knew that he was going to have to get some sleep that night if he was going to be able to do that again tomorrow. He was getting ready to slide back into the cab of the truck as he pulled off his shirt that had been soaked with sweat and threw it on the floor board. He caught a flash out of the corner of his eye and looked up in time to see the drapes being pulled shut of Kristen's second floor room. It seemed that he was being watched by more than one person as he left that day. He smiled and climbed into the truck and headed for home.

FIVE

There was not a sound except for the roar of the engine as Jackson pulled the sports car out on to the highway. He was hot and the white button down shirt that he was wearing seemed to be smothering him. He turned on the air conditioning and wiped a bead of sweat off of the side of his brow. He was a giant ball of nerves and was driving way too fast, but all he could think about was getting back to her. He had been working every single day since he had last seen her and he couldn't help but wonder what she would think of him now.

The town that he had grown up in was flying past him in a blur as he pointed his car up the highway toward the lake. He remembered making the same drive a thousand times that summer and each time it felt like it took an eternity in his old pickup truck. *You've come a long way my boy,* he thought to himself as he looked in the rearview mirror at his reflection. His mind told him to slow down, but his heart was pushing down the gas pedal as he came up past the hospital towards the house where he knew she'd be waiting.

Jackson kept his promise and was back at the lake house the next morning. A heavy fog had settled in all around the house and the lake looked like it was smoking. The air was thick and the sun, still hidden by the heavy cloud cover, had not started to do its damage. He made his way down the driveway and to the front door. He was less nervous today than yesterday about working for Ed, but far more nervous at the prospect of seeing Kristen. He knocked on the front door and it was a moment or two before someone answered. Sandy Taylor, Ed's wife, was there to greet Jackson instead.

"Hi, I'm Sandy," she said as she pulled the door open.

"Hi ma'am, nice to meet you," he said. "I'm Jackson Bryce." He stuck out his hand to offer to shake hers but she immediately pushed it out of the way and wrapped her arms around him in a hug. The gesture caught Jackson totally off guard and he only pulled himself together enough for a quick pat on her back before she was moving back towards the kitchen.

"Well Mr. Bryce, come on in. Ed is downstairs on the treadmill but if you want a cup of coffee or some breakfast he should be done in a minute."

"Ok thank you. A cup of coffee would be great," he replied. Heading back into the kitchen he was no less impressed today with the giant house than he was yesterday. He was even more glad that it had not been some kind of dream and that he had not somehow made the whole day up. He watched Sandy move to the pantry to get a cup for his coffee. It was easy to tell where Kristen got her looks. At almost fifty years old, she was still strikingly beautiful, and she had a smile and a demeanor that was warm and inviting. Like Kristen, she had dark tan skin and her eyes shown that same bright blue. Her brown hair was pulled up in the back, and though she had aged as everyone does, she was as beautiful as she had been twenty years ago. Where Ed was wired and ready to go all the time, she was laid back and relaxed. It was a fascinating balance and it was easy to see how they could play off of each other's strengths and weaknesses.

"Here you go," Sandy said, as she handed him the cup. "Would you like any cream or sugar?"

"Oh no ma'am, but thank you." He had never much cared for the taste of coffee but he remembered the smell from his childhood. It gave him a sense of comfort to hold the cup and smell the warm coffee smell making its way out of the "Number One Dad" mug that she handed to him.

"You aren't letting him work you too hard are you?" She asked as she moved around the kitchen counter to sit on one of the bar stools that was pulled up against the island countertop.

"Oh no, ma'am," he laughed. "It's not too bad, and it looks like the sun isn't going to come out for a while so I should be able to get a couple of hours in before it gets too hot."

"Well don't burn yourself up out there. If you get too hot during the day you feel free to just come in here and relax. I will make sure to tell Kristen to check on you from time to time to make sure you have plenty of water. If you get hungry, you just come right on in here and make yourself a sandwich."

"Thank you, ma'am, I really appreciate it."

"Did you meet Kristen yet?" she asked. Almost at once when she asked the question Jackson could feel his face go flush and he didn't know what to say. Before he had a chance to answer, Ed came up from the basement door.

"Well hey buddy," he called out as he shut the door behind himself. "Sorry if you've been waiting; I was trying to get a few minutes on the treadmill this morning."

"Oh no, I'm fine," Jackson replied. "Ms. Sandy had just poured me a cup of coffee right before you came up so I haven't been here long."

Ed's timing could not have been better for Jackson because he had not known what he was going to say when Sandy asked him about Kristen. He knew that she would have seen right through him. He did his best to not look right at her because he could still feel the intense red in his cheeks.

"Well when you finish up that cup of coffee I will show you what I've got for you today," Ed yelled out as he rounded the spiral staircase headed up to his bedroom.

"Well I am ready when you are," Jackson replied.

"Ok, I will be down in a second let me change clothes."

"Now I am serious about not letting him work you too hard," Sandy said to Jackson after her husband had made it upstairs. "If you don't feel like doing something or you get tired, you just stop. I don't want you getting tired and spending all of your summer break up here working. Be sure and get a little fun in."

Jackson smiled at the kindness in her words. His own mother was a tough and brash woman who was raising four kids by herself. She never took much time for such niceties. It wasn't that Jackson didn't understand what is mom was going through, but an occasional nice thought or hug would have gone a long way for him.

"Yes ma'am, thank you. I promise not too work too hard," Jackson said with a smile.

Sandy liked the way the boy looked when he smiled. Jackson's strong jaw bone and piercing eyes all seemed to melt away when he would smile. He had the kind of smile that required his entire face. It would start with a curl at the lips and almost all at once explode into a giant grin that involved a well balanced orchestration of eyes, brow, cheeks, and chin. She thought his smile made him look younger and less serious and was glad to see it spread across his face.

"Now are you going to be going to college in the fall?" Sandy asked. "Our Kristen is going to the University of Georgia. Not sure what she is going to do just yet. So where are you planning on going?"

Jackson hung is head sheepishly at the question. He felt sort of embarrassed and was not sure how to avoid an answer.

"Well, I don't think I will be going to college this fall, Ms. Sandy. We just really don't have the money and I kind of need to stay around here and help take care of my brothers." When he said it, a sadness came over his face, and the smile was immediately washed away. His eyes looked deep and longing as if he had already realized at the age of eighteen that he had gone as far as he would be able to go in this life. His face spoke of a longing that comes from knowing if he had been given different circumstances he would have been able to be anything he wanted to be. At that moment, he felt as low as he could feel. In so many ways he was afraid that he would always end up just doing work at someone else's house.

Sensing the change in the boy's mood, Sandy quickly changed the subject. Never being one to enjoy awkward silence she felt it best to not say anything else about it.

"Well maybe today if you get done with what you have to do around here, you could go out on the boat for a little while. I think after this fog burns off it is supposed to be a nice day."

"Yes ma'am, that would be fun. Maybe if I get done in time," Jackson replied. His tone was much more melancholy than it had been before. It was obvious to her that he was doing his best to hide it, but his feelings were just too close to the surface.

Just then Ed came making his way down the large staircase and back down into the kitchen. He had changed into some blue jeans and a button down shirt that seemed to swallow up his small frame.

"Ok buddy, let's head outside," he said it motioning to the front door. Jackson sprang up from his chair to follow him out.

When they got outside, the fog was still hanging everywhere and Ed moved over to the woods beside the house where three large trees lay down on the ground. Motioning to the downed trees he said, "Well buddy, I need you to help me get these trees cut up and the logs split and stacked. I know this sounds more like a winter job, but we need to get these trees cleared out so I can do some landscaping. The chainsaw is in the garage and there should be enough gas in it for you to be able to do all you will be able to do today. On my way back from the office I will get some more gas. You ever used a chainsaw?" he asked.

"Yes sir, I have a couple of times," Jackson replied. "Don't guess there's too much to it. Crank it up, point the sharp end at the tree, and don't cut your own leg off," he said with a smile.

"Yeah," Ed laughed. "Any legs cut off around here just get thrown in the lake so don't get any bright ideas that we might try and sew it back on."

Jackson laughed. "I will keep that in mind, Doc."

Jackson surveyed the job that was laid out in front of him. It would take him a week to get all of the trees cut up split and stacked. He felt tired already but he knew that the money for the job would be nice and so he just smiled and said, "Well I better get to it. Looks like I have a lot of work laid out for me."

"Yeah it should take you a few days to get all of this done," Ed answered. "Don't feel like you have to get it all done in one shot." With that, Ed turned and headed back toward the house. "Well I need to grab my stuff and head to the hospital, I think Sandy is heading toward town in a little while, so like yesterday if you need anything just call me or find Kristen."

As he said it he disappeared into the house. *Kristen.* Just the thought of her name made Jackson nervous and excited. He had closed his eyes in bed the night before trying to think of what he would say if he was left with just Kristen again today. He didn't want to seem interested, but more importantly he didn't want to seem nervous when she came around. He knew that this was going to be easier said than done. He looked up to Kristen's second floor window where he knew she was probably still asleep and he wondered if she had even given him a second thought at all.

He was in the garage getting the chainsaw and axe together when he heard Ed's car crank up and pull out of the driveway. Gathering up everything he would need, Jackson walked out of the garage and up towards the fallen trees in time to see Ed's fire red convertible go speeding down the road in front of the house. *What a ride,* he thought to himself as he laid the chainsaw and axe down next to the tree where he would start.

SIX

Kristen was still in the rocking chair on the back porch, but her rocking had become slower and less frantic. Thinking back on that summer gave her chill bumps. She was left with a feeling of childish excitement that was normally reserved for birthday parties and Christmas mornings. She could remember everything about him and every conversation that they had had. Every moment was special to her but she had done a good job of pushing it out of her mind since he left. For a couple of months after he was gone she convinced herself that he would be back, after a couple of years it seemed that it would never happen. She ran her hand down her chest to feel her necklace hanging in its place. It had become a memoir of so many good times and a constant reminder of time gone by.

The sun was working down in the sky and the cool air and the rocking of the chair were making her eyes grow heavy. She couldn't help but wonder what was keeping Jackson. She knew that he was never late for anything. Looking at her watch for the hundredth time, she settled back in to a slower rock as her mind retraced the events of that summer.

She was still sound asleep in her bed when she heard the chainsaw fire up. She knew that it was Jackson and she jumped out of bed with an uncharacteristic spring in her step and went over to her window to see where he was and what he was doing. He was already at work on one of the trees and she couldn't help but be impressed by how someone her age who should be out enjoying some time off from school was out working so early in the morning. As he moved from section to section of the tree, his arms tensed as he moved through each cut. She got lost in each movement that he made with the chainsaw. She could see the muscles in his forearms as he moved through the tree and the rhythm of the chainsaw felt sort of hypnotic as she watched him work. She had been standing there in the window with the curtains pulled back looking outside for about five minutes when she heard a voice from behind her.

"What you lookin at?" The voice came from the door. She turned to see her little sister Alyson standing at the door in her night gown.

"Nothing," Kristen replied. She dropped the curtain back in place and moved away from the window.

"What are you doing up so early?" Kristen asked surprised to see the sleepy looking youngster up so early.

Rubbing her eyes, the six-year-old shot back, "I start bible school today." Alyson, like Kristen and her mother, had dark skin and bright blue eyes. Like her father she had the small stature and wiry frame.

Kristen had forgotten about the bible school and almost as quickly as she remembered she realized that she would be there all day alone with Jackson. Her mom had volunteered to help teach one of the classes which meant that she would be gone all day with Alyson. Thinking about being there alone with Jackson made her nervous. She knew that if he needed anything that she was the only one there he could ask. She moved back over to the window and pulled back the curtains to see what he was doing. The chainsaw was still running wide open, and he was still hard at work. Feeling as if he were being watched, Jackson took his attention off the tree he was cutting in time to see the blinds dropped quickly back into place. Kristen felt sick at her stomach. He had seen her watching him which would only help in making her feel more awkward if they were forced to talk.

Kristen turned to head downstairs and as she moved past Alyson she said, "Come on, kiddo, let's go get some breakfast."

"What were you looking at?" The little girl asked.

"Nothing, now do you want some breakfast or not?"

"Yeah I want some breakfast," Alyson replied. "But I sure would like to know what you were looking at."

Kristen ignored the comment and headed down towards the kitchen. Grabbing Alyson's hand in case she got the bright idea to go to the window, she led her downstairs to fix some breakfast. Sandy was surprised to see the two coming down the stairs so early. She wasn't used to seeing her girls before lunch time.

"Well what has you girls up and moving so early this morning?" their mom asked. As she asked, she heard Jackson outside rev up the chainsaw as he moved through another section of the tree. "I should have brought Jackson by here years ago if I would have thought that chainsaw would be what it took to get you out of bed," Sandy said with a laugh.

The girls failed to find the humor in it and quickly dismissed it as they moved over to the fridge to find some breakfast.

"Alyson, you need to hurry and get ready. If you can wait to eat breakfast we will stop in town. Kristen, you're on your own darling. I have to run some errands before bible school starts."

Always excited to get to go out and eat, Alyson ran back upstairs to get in the shower.

"That Jackson seems to be a nice boy," Sandy said.

"Yeah, he seems nice enough," Kristen replied with her eyes looking straight down at the floor.

"It's a shame a smart young man like that isn't going to college in the fall, but maybe something will work out for him. Did you guys go to high school together?"

"No," Kristen replied. "He went to Northwest High across town. I think he played football for them."

"Oh I didn't think that you guys knew each other," Sandy replied.

No trust me, mom. If I knew him you would have heard about it, Kristen thought to herself as she pulled some eggs out of the fridge for breakfast.

"Well if he needs anything today you get it for him, ok? And go out and check on him from time to time and make sure he has plenty of water. I don't want him working too hard today. I think it is going to get pretty hot."

"Yeah, I will check on him." *Great, now I have to go out there and check on him.* The idea of having to go out there after being caught looking out the window at him made her nervous, and it was a job she would like to get out of.

"I mean it now, don't forget," Sandy shot back. "It is going to be hot and that boy is going to need some water. You make sure he drinks plenty of water. Your father will work that poor boy to death and I just don't want him spending his whole summer break up here working all the time."

As she rambled on and on and headed towards the laundry room, Kristen had already tuned her out. Her mom was always ranting on and on about something. It wasn't that she was mad about anything or upset. She would start in on one topic and it seemed like everything she said reminded her of something else and before you knew it she had been talking for an hour and you weren't exactly sure what you had just heard.

As her mom's voice began to fade into the background, Kristen cracked a couple of eggs into a pan that she had just thrown on to the stove. Reaching into the fridge for some orange juice, she almost jumped out of her skin when she shut the door to see Jackson standing there behind it.

"Oh my God, Jack, you scared me!"

"Sorry. I'm sorry. I didn't mean to creep up on you all *Friday the Thirteenth* style. I just needed to get a rag or something from you. I don't mean to bother you."

"Oh no, it's not a bother," she responded. She turned away from him to look at the microwave. She could see her reflection and tried her best to fix her hair that had taken on a life of its own. *I am so glad I decided to wear my cute matching pajamas.*

"So what do you need a rag for?" Kristen asked, pulling the eggs off the stove. She moved over to the drawer beside the sink to find a rag.

"Oh, it's nothing," he replied. "I kind of cut myself and I just needed a rag."

"Cut yourself?" She turned to see a large tear in his jeans just below the right knee. "What did you do?"

"Oh, it's nothing," he replied trying to calm her down. "I am fine. It is not that bad of a cut, I promise. The old blue jeans took most of the damage."

"Well, sit down," she said moving past him to pull out a chair from the kitchen table. "Sit down."

He moved over to the chair and took a seat. There was some blood on the outside of the blue jeans but Kristen could not tell how bad the cut was.

"Mom!" She yelled. "Momma!"

Sandy came out of the laundry room with a basket of clothes in her hand and a panicked look on her face.

"What?" She asked not really sure that she wanted to know what the fuss was about so early in the morning.

"Jackson cut himself."

"Well boy, what did you go and do that for?" she said. Her tone was not a joking tone. It truly sounded like she wanted to know why in the world anyone would cut their own leg.

"I was moving through a part of the tree and it kicked back on me. I wasn't really paying attention. It's my own stupid fault." He felt so embarrassed at the fuss that was being made.

"Well we need to get you to the hospital right now," Sandy said. "We need to get you fixed up."

"Oh please, don't call the hospital," Jackson pleaded. "And whatever you do please don't tell Ed. I don't want him thinking I can't work out here. He might think I am some kind of a dumb kid that can't manage to do a little work without cutting his own leg. Please don't call the hospital." His tone was scared and his eyes had a kind of frantic look.

Kristen wasn't sure what to do so she went over to the pantry to get a glass for some water for him.

"Well, we will see what it looks like and if it isn't too serious than maybe we can just fix it here," Sandy said. She could sense that he was truly worried and she knew that Ed might see this accident as a sign that this boy couldn't handle it, and would ask him not to come back. She had enjoyed their conversation that morning and she could tell he was a good boy, and she knew he must be embarrassed about the whole thing.

"Kristen, you get some stuff to clean up the cut. I am going to run next door. Ms. Johnston has some bandage stuff at her house. I will be right back," Sandy said as she moved out the front door to go across the street.

Kristen looked at Jackson but she did her best to not look at his eyes. She looked down at the large tear in the blue jeans, and she went over to the sink to wet the rag that she had pulled out from the drawer. She shyly made her way back over to Jackson still doing her best to not make eye contact with him. As she came by the counter and moved over to the kitchen table where Jackson was sitting, she grabbed a pair of scissors that someone had left there. Doing her best to not look at him, she got down on the floor and slid over next to the cut leg. It was the closest she had been to him and she was trying her best to look calm and collected. She grabbed the hole in the jeans with one hand and the scissors that she had just gotten with the other.

"Wait, what are you doing?" Jackson asked pushing back at her hand. His face went flushed as they touched.

"I was going to cut the pants leg off so we could get to it to fix it," she said. She was startled by how quickly he had moved to stop her but how gently he had moved her hand.

"What would you do that for?" he asked. "Can't I just roll my pants leg up?"

"You could if you would have cut your ankle" she replied. "But you went and cut up by your knee so I need to cut of the leg of your blue jeans." As she said it she moved back to cut the jeans off, and again he moved to stop her.

"Well I need these pants," he said. "I can't just go cutting the leg off of a perfectly good pair of pants."

"Well what's more important, Jackson; cutting off the leg of your pants so I can fix your leg or saving a pair of blue jeans?" Kristen asked very matter of factly. She was sure that it was a strong enough argument and that he would give in. With that she moved in again with the scissors to cut off the pant leg.

Stopping her, and with a frustrated look on his face, he replied, "This cut on my leg will heal, but if I cut off a leg of my blue jeans my mom will kill me, and you don't get better from someone killing you."

Frustrated and not sure what to do, Kristen slid away from him. "Well, how do you expect me to get to that cut if you won't cooperate?"

"Well I could just roll the pants up," he said. He bent down to start rolling the jeans from the bottom up. He had only gotten about half way up his calf when he realized the jeans had gone as far as they would go. The wrangler blue jeans he was wearing didn't have a wide enough leg to get it pulled up over his knee. Frustrated, he pulled his pants back down around his boots. As he rolled his pants back down, he chuckled to himself, humored by the situation he had put himself in. As he laughed, and started to relax a little bit, he looked up from his blue jeans to see Kristen looking back at him. It was the first time that their eyes had truly met. It was a moment. A moment that they had stolen away from everything going on all around them and everyone that they knew. It was a moment to share only with each other. Jackson stared into her eyes and he couldn't move. The sting that had been resonating from his leg was a distant thought. He had never believed in things like love at first sight, or feeling butterflies, or whatever it was called, but he quickly changed his mind. He was lost in her face, and he kept tracing the line that ran from her nose to her lips. It was the kind of moment that should be allowed to go on forever, but never does. The world is jealous of moments like these and so often they are stolen too soon.

Kristen couldn't help but stare back. Her mind was screaming at her to look away but her eyes were telling her to stay fast. She didn't move and for a moment or two she was not sure if she had remembered to breath. She stared into his deep green eyes watching the sadness that she had seen in them before begin to wash away. There was something different there now. Staring back at him, time seemed to stop when, in truth, only seconds had passed.

They both sat there for a minute, not knowing what to do. Before either one of them could move, Sandy came busting back through the door.

"Ok son, let's get you fixed up. I went and got some bandages from Ms. Johnston, so all we have to do is wrap you up and you will be good to go. Lets get that pant leg cut off of there," she said reaching for the scissors in Kristen's hand.

"Don't even try it, Momma," she said, handing over the scissors. "I tried to do it a second ago and he bout had a cow, and he can't get it pulled up over his knee," she added quickly. It was followed with an *I told you so* look that she flashed back at Jackson.

Without even missing a beat, Sandy looked at Jackson and said, "Well, pull your pants down."

As soon as she said it, Jackson's face turned fire engine red and the first thing he did was to look at Kristen. When their eyes met, her face turned red, too, and the tension in the air quickly became so thick it could be cut with a knife. Sandy saw Jackson's face go red, and she knew she had to get Kristen out of there.

"Alright Kristen, to your room," she said. "I don't want Jackson feeling funny because you are standing here. Now go on."

Kristen was almost thankful for the break in tension and gave no argument as she headed around the corner and back upstairs to her room. She couldn't explain the moment she had just had there with Jackson and it left her with a strange feeling. It was something that she had never experienced before.

For Jackson, the situation was not getting much better. He went from the awkward tension with Kristen there in the kitchen to having to take his pants off in front of a woman that he had just met at breakfast.

"Now Jackson, don't be embarrassed; I was a nurse for many years. It won't be anything I haven't seen before."

As she said it, Jackson stood up from the chair, unbuttoned his pants and pulled them down around his ankles. The situation was almost more than he could bear, and he couldn't tell if it was because his pants were around his ankles, because Kristen had just given him an incredible look, or the fact that he was loosing blood every second, but he felt like throwing up.

The moment his pants went around his ankles, he quickly covered himself with his hands and sat back down in the chair. He was glad that he had picked a half way descent set of underwear out of the drawer that morning as he sat there in the kitchen with them exposed to the world. It was not how he had envisioned his day going.

Sandy quickly went to work on the cut that he had made on his leg. Even though she had not been a nurse since Kristen was much younger, it was obvious that she still had the touch, and more importantly the strong stomach.

"Well it doesn't look so bad," she said as she cleaned the cut with the wet rag that Kristen had left lying on the counter. "I don't think you would need any stitches, but if you feel like going to the doctor later you let me know, and I will take you down there." She pulled out some disinfectant and rubbed down the cut. Jackson winced at the pain but only for a second. He didn't want to seem weak and was really glad that Sandy had made Kristen leave.

Quietly, Jackson asked, "You aren't going to tell Ed, are you? I don't want him thinking I am some kind of an idiot that can't work a chainsaw. Plus, I really need this work, Ms. Sandy."

"Well, I think we can keep it between us if you promise to be careful from now on," she replied. She knew that her husband was a good man, but he had little patience for mistakes or accidents. He would have viewed the whole thing as a sign of incompetence, and would have probably asked him to not come back. He wouldn't have done it to be mean but he figured that there wasn't much room for mistakes in his type of work, so he didn't leave much room for mistakes with other people.

Jackson smiled when she said it, and relaxed a little bit as she began to wrap the bandage around the cut. "Thank you Ms Sandy. I really mean it. Thank you."

"It's not a problem, Jackson; just be careful."

"Oh I will; I promise."

"Ok I think that's got it. You can get those pants back on," she said with a wink.

Jackson sprung up from the chair and pulled his blue jeans back up and headed toward the door. "I better get back to work. I lost some time, but if I keep at it I can get caught back up. Thanks again."

"Not a problem, Jack. Just be careful."

"Yes ma'am, I promise."

Jackson headed back out the door with only a slight limp from the cut and went right back to work. He felt stupid for causing such a commotion, and was upset about the fact that he had lost some time. As he cranked back up the chainsaw and went back to work, he looked back up at Kristen's second floor window. This time Kristen was standing in the window, but when Jackson looked she didn't try to hide. She stood there with the drapes pulled to the side and stared down at him. She felt like Juliet looking down at her Romeo, only her Romeo had a chainsaw.

He flashed his large toothy grin at her and went back to work. His mind was racing from earlier and he couldn't believe the fireworks he had felt. He had never felt anything like that and he wasn't sure exactly what it all meant. He wanted to get back up there and talk to her but he knew that his work came first. He was moving down the log cut after cut when he saw the garage door open and Sandy's car pull out onto the driveway. She pulled up next to where Jackson was working and rolled down her window to call out to him.

"If you need anything, Kristen is inside. Just go right on in and get what you need. Make yourself at home, and don't work too hard; it is supposed to get really hot today."

"Ok thanks, Ms. Sandy," Jackson replied.

As he said it she rolled up the window and headed out of the driveway and on to the street. He could see Alyson sitting in the backseat and he gave her a quick wave. She stuck her tongue out and pressed her face against the window and he watched her hold the pose until the car was out of sight. He couldn't help but think what an incredibly nice woman Sandy was, and he smiled as he went back to work. Catching a glimpse of the tear in his pants leg, his mind traced back to his moment with Kristen there in the kitchen. The sun started to climb up higher in the sky burning off the early morning fog but the heat didn't seem to bother him. Back to his work, the events of the morning raced at him like a blur. His stomach felt queasy at the thought of having to pull his pants down there in the middle of the kitchen. Despite it all, he couldn't help but smile as he looked back up to the second floor window to see her standing there again.

SEVEN

The day had started out with a thick fog, and the air had been heavy. The sun began to climb higher and the fog began to move away leaving behind nothing but the heat. It was sometime after lunch and Jackson had finally finished cutting the three large trees into sections that he would now have to begin splitting and stacking. The heat had started to get to him, and the pain from the cut on his leg had started to nag him more and more as the hours passed. The sunlight forced his eyes to squint closed, and the air seemed dead with no breeze blowing. The shirt that he had on was drenched in sweat and it was covered in saw dust that had been sprayed all over him as he used the chainsaw. He wrestled up the first log that was to be split and he stood it up on end. The axe was large and heavy and he knew immediately why Ed had left the job to him. Despite his broad shoulders and large arms, the axe still seemed massive. He stood the logs upright and picked up the oversized axe that he had brought up from the garage and began splitting them one after another. He had settled into a rhythm and was beginning to lose track of time as he stood up log after log and then sent it falling back to the ground in halves with one strong swing. Completely entranced by the rhythm of his work, he didn't see Kristen come out of the house carrying the large glass of ice water.

"Brought you some water," she said as he brought the axe up high over his head. When she said it, he jumped and the axe almost went flying out of his hand.

"Oh man, you scared me," he said. "I didn't hear you come out." He had a startled look on his face, and he was a little embarrassed that he had jumped like he did.

"Sorry, I just thought you might like some water."

She had only been out there for just a minute but she could feel the intense heat of the day, and she wondered how he was able to stay at it for so long. It had turned into the kind of day that is so hot that the heat feels like it is coming from all sides. The ground even felt like it was giving off heat as she stood there holding the glass that had begun to sweat all over her hand.

"Thank you so much," he said in a winded voice. He reached out awkwardly to grab the water, and kept his eyes focused squarely on the cup as he took it from her. His mouth was dry from the heat and the saw dust, and he could feel the cold stream of water run down his throat and into his belly. He hadn't realized how thirsty he was and drank the water down quickly.

"Thank you," he said again. "That hit the spot."

"So how much more are you going to do today?" she asked.

"Well, I am gonna work till I can't swing this axe anymore and then I am gonna split about ten more," he said with a sheepish grin.

"I don't know how you do it. I don't think I could take this heat for too long."

"Oh you'd be surprised how much you can take if you put your mind to doing it," he said. "I can think of a lot of things I would rather be doing, but work is work, so I got to get it done." He handed her back the water glass and took back up the axe. Steadying another log, he raised the axe back up high over his head and let the blade come crashing down on the log. It split cleanly all the way down and he kicked the two halves out of the way to grab another one.

Kristen watched as he repeated the process over and over. She wanted to talk but felt like she was interrupting a delicate rhythm that he had struck between himself and the axe. She simply watched as he stood another log up to split it quickly with a blow of the axe.

"How did you learn to do that?" she asked.

"Do what, split a log? Oh I don't know if you actually ever learn how to do it. I figure you just stand it up and then swing. I reckon the pointy end just needs to go into the wood." When he said it, he flashed a smile at her that took up his entire face.

"Well that sounds simple enough," she replied. "I bet I could probably do that."

"You want to give it a try?" he asked, offering the large axe over to her.

"Oh no, no. I think I better leave it to the professionals." When she said it she turned back to head into the house.

"Yeah that's probably a good idea, leave it to the professionals."

"I mean I wouldn't want to go cutting my leg up or anything," she said back to him. She turned to give him a grin and then walked back into the house strutting like she had just won a battle.

He laughed as he watched her disappear back through the front door and steadied up another log.

Sticking her head back out the door she called to him, "Hey, I am gonna make a sandwich, you hungry?"

"Yeah, a little but don't go to any trouble for me."

"Oh no trouble," she said, "I will be back out later. Try not to pass out from hunger between now and then," she said as she disappeared behind the door.

Kristen made her way into the house holding the empty glass she had taken back from him, smiling proudly at herself for her sharp comeback. She had wanted to stay out there with him longer but she wasn't sure what she would have said. More importantly, she didn't want to get in the way, or make him feel weird by standing there watching him work. Earlier that morning when she had been sitting on the kitchen floor trying to fix the cut on his leg, she had felt an explosion all over her body when he looked at her. Just thinking about it sent a chill running up her back and she wondered if he had felt something too.

She looked at the clock on the wall to check the time and figured that it was getting time to fix something for lunch. She knew if she was hungry that he must be starving so she went into the kitchen to fix a couple of sandwiches. Pulling the stuff from the refrigerator to make the sandwiches, her movements became more excited as she began to think about Jackson. There was something about him that she couldn't put her finger on. The way that he moved, the way that he smiled, the power that he showed each time he swung down with the axe, all made her feel less like a girl and more like a woman. His presence there in the house had awoken a part of her that she had not known before. When he looked at her, it made her want his touch more than anything in the world. The thought seemed almost ridiculous to her because they were perfect strangers, and aside from the couple of words they had spoken with each other today she didn't know anything about him. Maybe the appeal of this man was because he was such a mystery. She had known the guys she went to school with her entire life. She knew everything about them. She remembered when they went through those awkward middle school years, and she remembered first dances and first kisses, but with Jackson it was a total mystery. The only thing she knew about Jackson was from what she had seen in the paper a couple of times. In the fall, Saturday morning headlines from the local paper always had something about him. She knew little about football but she knew enough to know that if you got your name in the paper you had to at least be pretty good.

She had managed to throw together a couple of sandwiches and after wrapping them up in a napkin and fixing another big glass of water, she headed back outside to bring him some lunch.

Leaving the house and rounding the corner to where he had been working, she saw him setting up another log. With the same power the axe came crashing down and the log fell to the ground. Soaked in sweat and covered in sawdust, his shirt had become sticky and itchy. As she got closer she saw that he had taken it off and hung it on a branch next to where he was working. She stopped moving closer and watched as he righted another log and grabbed his axe to make another swing. Every muscle of his torso was coursing with blood and the veins on his arms traced down his biceps and down onto his forearms. His stomach was tight and as he raised the axe above his head his abs flexed along with his shoulders to bring the axe hurdling down. She could tell that his muscles were not manufactured in any weight room. He had earned them from thousands of hours of work just like this. Even though the work seemed hard, he appeared content and the worry in his eyes had been replaced with an intense focus. Hanging from his neck was a medallion of some sort on an old chain. It looked old, and not just because of the tarnish but the way it was made and the chain it was on. Each movement he made the necklace moved with him always settling back down in the middle of his chest. Moving over to where he was working, she called out to him.

"Brought you a sandwich if you're still hungry, and I figured you were probably thirsty for another glass of water."

"Oh wow, you didn't have to do that. Thanks a lot."

He hadn't realized that she was out there, and immediately reached for his shirt as she came walking towards him. Wrestling back on the soaking wet shirt, she couldn't help but be impressed at his modesty. Most guys she had gone to school with worked out just so they could strut around the pool, and would never think to put on a shirt because a girl had walked over.

"I hope you like ham," she said, handing him the sandwich and the glass of water. "It's all we had in the house."

"Oh yeah, ham is fine. I could eat a horse right now," he replied.

He took the sandwich and the water eagerly. He grabbed one of the logs that he had not split yet and turned it upright and sat down. The light green shirt and the khaki shorts that she had on made her dark tan skin stand out even more. He tried not to stare, and instead focused on unwrapping the napkin from the sandwich. He was starving and he was glad that she had thought to make him something to eat.

"You gonna join me?"

"Um . . . yeah I could do that," she replied, thankful that he had asked.

She began looking around for a place to sit. Jackson immediately hopped up from the log he was sitting on and offered it to her.

"Oh thank you, giving up your log for me?" she said with a smile.

"I figure it's the least I could do since you brought me this sandwich."

As she made herself comfortable on the log, he grabbed another log and sat it up and took his seat on it facing her.

"Well it wasn't any trouble," she said. "Making sandwiches is a little easier than what you've been doing all day."

"Yeah but your sandwich is all part of the process. Without your sandwich I would have been out here having to eat grass or bugs to stay alive. You can't do much log splitting on a full belly of grass," he said with a laugh and a light tone in his voice.

"No, we wouldn't want that," she said, surprised that the serious young man had a playful side at all. "So how's the leg?"

"Oh this old thing," he replied, tugging at the tear in his blue jeans. "Feels okay. I think all it needed to heal up all the way was a good ham sandwich," he said winking at her. "So what do you do in that house all day?" he asked.

"Well I would say sleep in, but there was a loud chainsaw roaring outside my room first thing this morning," she said teasingly. "I read mostly. Sometimes I read for hours at a time. I go down to the dock sometimes and hang out, and sometimes I take the boat out for a ride. I don't know. Just hang out I guess."

"Man, sounds like a pretty good day." He was jealous of the luxury that she enjoyed. It would be great to be able to sleep in late and play all day. He wondered what a day like that would even feel like. He had been working since he could remember on almost everyday that he had free, so her laid back style made him a little jealous.

"Well it's alright, I guess. I get bored a lot. Mom and Alyson are usually off somewhere and Dad is always working. I just kind of sit around here and come up with things to do." She wished that her dad would give her more responsibility and take her a little more seriously. It was getting close to time for her to head off to college and she was still, in so many ways, being treated like she was headed to high school instead. She wished she could just pick up the axe and work instead of sitting in the house reading all of those books.

Taking down another bite of his sandwich, Jackson took a large drink of his ice water. Having a little company was nice and he wished that he could talk to her all day.

"So where did you go to school?" she asked, even though she already knew the answer. She was doing her best to make some small talk.

"I went to Northwest. It's not a bad school like some people think. The teachers are great and Ms. Landler the lunch lady always gave me extra peanut butter cookies so I guess it was alright," he said. "It's not a fancy school but I never figured myself for a fancy type of guy. What about you?"

"Yeah, I never figured you for a fancy type of guy either," she said laughing.

"No, I meant what about you, like where did you go to school?"

"I know what you meant I was just messing with you," she said. "I went to Cartersville City School," she said. "It was a good school I guess, but no peanut butter cookies."

"Yeah, I've always been a sucker for peanut butter cookies," he said smiling back at her. "If it ever comes up I will ask Ms. Landler for an extra cookie, she lives two houses down from me."

"Well that would be sweet," she replied. She smiled thinking that Jackson was probably the kind of guy who would follow up on his offer. She thoroughly expected to see him come strolling up with a bag full of peanut butter cookies one day.

"Don't you get hot out here?" she asked.

"Don't you get bored sitting in that house?" he replied back with a smile.

They both smiled and sat there quietly enjoying the light breeze that had begun to work its way up from the lake and through the trees where they were sitting.

"So I guess um, your boyfriend is probably gonna miss you in the fall when you leave to go to school," he said quickly looking down pretending to be studying his sandwich.

"Oh, I don't have a boyfriend."

When she said it Jackson did his best to hide the smile that was forming in the corners of his mouth. They both stared down at the ground shuffling their feet trying to think of what to say next.

"So I guess your girlfriend must hate that you are up here working all day instead of spending time with her," she said still looking at the ground.

"Oh I definitely don't have a girlfriend," he replied quickly. "I have never been too good at those things. It seems my brain and my heart don't always see eye to eye on how stuff like that should go so I manage to steer clear of it when I can."

"Oh, I see, love on the rocks, huh," she said laughing.

"Yeah, love on the rocks," he smiled. Jackson had never really dated at all. He had been working since he was young and between school and work he had never really found the time or money to date.

Kristen did her best not to look at him when he mentioned that he didn't have a girlfriend. She wasn't sure if she would have been able to hide her disappointment if he would have told her otherwise. She could feel an attraction to him that she could not explain. He seemed so strong and confident sitting there on his log. His posture and his strength impressed her. He appeared to have a confidence about him that was not like the arrogance that she had seen from guys that her father worked with or that she ran into at the country club. His confidence seemed more like defiance. It was as if he was daring any man in the room who thought he was better to try.

"I mean what about you? I can figure why a dumb-dumb like me wouldn't have somebody, but you seem like the kind of girl that would have to beat 'em off with a stick."

"Oh really? Well I appreciate it but to be honest I am horrible at that kind of stuff too. It's not cause my brain and my heart don't see eye to eye. It's more like my brain doesn't factor in at all and I do that whole girlie emotional thing. I try to talk myself out of it but I mostly just end up crying or yelling."

"Yeah, I understand. Sounds an awful lot like my sister."

"Oh you have a sister?"

Pausing to swallow his bite of sandwich he replied, "Yeah, a twin actually. Mom says we split a brain. I figure if I would have just been one person and gotten the whole thing, I really would be a sharp fella. I think it's that whole half a brain thing that gets me in trouble." He laughed a little at his own joke as he leaned down to take another bite of his sandwich.

"Wow, what's it like having a twin?"

"I don't know; what's it like not having one?" he replied. "People are always asking me that and I never know what to say. They always ask me if we are identical, too. For most folks, I don't get into the whole boys have 'a this' and girls have 'a that' conversation."

When he said it, laughter burst from her mouth and she didn't try to contain it as she laughed harder and harder. He didn't seem like the joking type when she first met him but she could see his sense of humor creeping up from its hiding spot as they talked. His posture was getting more relaxed. He had been so rigid and as he told his jokes and made his wise crack comebacks, she could see the tension in his muscles begin to dissolve.

"Yeah girls have 'a this' and boys have 'a that'," she laughed again.

"I have a couple of brothers, too," he added. "They are both several years younger than I am, but they are good guys. They wear me out sometimes. Your little sister seems like she could be a handful," he said. He then told her how she had stuck her tongue out at him as they pulled out of the driveway earlier that morning.

"Yeah, that's Alyson for you. She can be a little brat. She says that boys are evil, which is probably why she stuck her tongue out at you."

"Do you think boys are evil," he asked sheepishly.

"Absolutely. I don't get caught up in that whole love till the end of time thing. Boys only want one thing and they will tell you whatever you need to hear to get it. So yeah, boys are evil."

"Man, hate to hear that. I happen to be a boy, ya know."

"Really? Could have fooled me," she said with a smile.

"Cold, that's just cold," he said. "So there's no prince charming out there waiting for you, huh? No knight on a big white horse to come whisk you away into the sunset? I thought that's what girls wanted."

"Girls only want that stuff cause most girls just want to feel safe. The only thing Prince Charming and the Knight on a white horse have in common is that they can protect you. They can make you feel like you are safe. It's not bad to want to be protected is it? I mean wouldn't you want that?" She looked up at him waiting for his answer. She felt flustered and reached up to wipe the sweat that was beading up on her forehead.

"Yeah, but who protects the knight, or prince charming," he asked.

"If he hurts my feelings or cheats on me, nothing can protect him," she said. When she did she rubbed her hands together in a maniacal way and let out an evil laugh.

Jackson could not contain himself from the laughter that came roaring up out of his mouth. As she sat there on her log, cackling her evil laugh, Jackson laughed until his stomach hurt. She was laughing along with him and it took several minutes before they were able to get their composure.

The thing that surprised Jackson was that he couldn't help but feel comfortable around her. He had made a lifetime out of silence, and had learned not to laugh and not to cry. He gave very little of himself to people because he had always believed that it could only get him hurt. Sitting there on the two logs in the middle of the woods by the lake he could feel a new and strange desire to let her see him. He wanted her to know him, and the strangeness of it all was that he couldn't explain why.

"Well sounds to me like Prince Charming better watch his step," Jackson said with a smile.

"Yeah, you better believe it. If prince charming thinks the fire breathing dragon is bad, he ain't seen nothing till I get a hold of him," Kristen said laughing.

They both laughed and then it got quiet.

"Too bad there is no prince charming, or knights in shining armor," she said bringing her eyes up to meet his.

"There might be. Don't give up hope just yet. There just might be a prince charming out there somewhere."

EIGHT

Jackson Bryce was still flying up the highway toward the lake and looking at the clock on the dash every second. He had a strange feeling in his stomach as he made the turn up Wilderness Camp Road toward the lake. He had been down this road many times before, but this time there was something different. For the first time since he had left he began to feel happy. He was happy in the thought that at the end of this road meant no more goodbyes. At the end of this road meant no more lonely nights, and no more regrets. For the first time in his life the load on his shoulders seemed gone forever.

He smiled as the car took the turns at faster and faster speeds. Whether she knew it or not, Kristen had not just given him an unforgettable summer, she had given him dreams. He remembered every detail of that summer and as he drove his mind began to replay the afternoon that changed his life forever.

Jackson and Kristen were still sitting on the logs staring at each other. Kristen's gaze was fixed on him, his dark greens eyes seemed to be piercing through her. He made her feel hot and excited, and scared, and happy all at the same time. She didn't want to feel this way about a guy she barely knew but with every word that he said she felt a little closer to him.

"Well when you find prince charming will you tell him where I live," she said.

When she said it they both fell into laughter. The tension that had been building disappeared and he watched her as she laughed at her own joke.

"Yeah, I will let him know, and I will tell him to bring an axe, cause it looks like I am gonna need some help," he said looking at his watch. "Man, your dad is not going to be happy with me if I don't get this stuff done. I should probably get back to work."

"Oh don't you worry about dad," she replied. "He may seem like a tough guy but I can melt him like butter. Plus, I don't want you over doing yourself, what with your extensive leg injuries and all."

"Oh you can't say a word about that. Please don't say anything to him about that."

"Oh I won't; it will be our little secret. Oh, and mom and Alyson's, too."

He knew it would only be a matter of time before one of them slipped up and said something; he just hoped that he had done enough good work by then so that Ed would want to keep him around.

Jackson took another bite of his sandwich and a drink from his water glass while she launched into story after story. He was enjoying the conversation and as she went on and on talking about her school, and a trip to the beach that she took the summer before, and this guy that she used to date but didn't date anymore because he had turned out to be a creep, he just stared at her and listened. He liked the way her mouth formed around her teeth when she would smile, and he would wait patiently through the stories for a part that she thought was funny.

He didn't get a word in edgewise for about fifteen minutes, but he didn't really mind. He was losing track of time and he was getting behind on his work but he would trade all of the money he would make for a few more afternoons like that one.

Pulling him back in from his gaze, she asked, "So, if you don't mind me asking, why do you come out here and work all day? Wouldn't you rather be out somewhere enjoying your summer?"

Jackson was taken aback by the questions. He was embarrassed to have to answer them. He looked down at the ground and paused for a second.

"I mean you don't have to say anything," she interjected. "I was just making talk. I didn't mean to make you uncomfortable or anything."

"Oh no, it's ok," he said. "I um . . . well my family doesn't have much money. In fact, I would say that we have next to nothing. I work out here cause we need the money. My dad left when I was just a kid so we have just been doing what we can to make it. It's not easy, but nothing worth a darn is."

When he said it, he brought his eyes up to meet hers. Neither one of them moved for a minute or two, until she spoke.

Staring back into his eyes she said quietly, "Is that why your eyes look so sad?" As soon as she said it she regretted the question. She had not meant to offend him but the look on his face told her that it had. Her mouth dropped open as if she couldn't believe that she had said it herself and she wished she could have pulled back the words. It wasn't the kind of question that you ask a person the first time you eat lunch with them.

He looked back down at his half eaten sandwich. The silence was killing her and the world seemed to quit turning. When he looked up he looked up with a different look in his eyes than he had had a moment earlier. It wasn't a look of anger but more a look of resolve. He sat upright on the log that he had been using as a seat.

"What would you know about sadness?"

His tone was without any feeling at all. There was no joy or hate in his words. It was only numbness. It was a numbness that had taken over his mind years ago, and it was a numbness that pushed him through each and every day.

She stared back at him not knowing what to say. The breeze had stopped blowing and the sun felt even hotter on her face. She could feel the sweat beginning to crop up on her forehead and the glare of daylight forced her to squint her eyes. She was taken aback by how quickly his mood had changed. She had seen a softer more joking side of him start to emerge only to go screaming back into hiding.

"I'm sorry, I'm sorry. That was wrong; I don't know why I said that. I am just a stupid girl. Forget that I said that." While she was apologizing, she stood from the log she was sitting on and began to move toward the door. Grabbing up her napkin, she hung her head down and kept saying over and over, "I'm sorry. I didn't mean to say something like that." She looked back up at him to see if she could see what he was thinking but his face was like stone and he was sitting straight and stiff on his log. He didn't move a muscle as she made her way back toward the door. She thanked him for eating lunch with her but he didn't move. She finally made her way back toward the door and reached out for the handle to go back inside.

He wanted to stop her but he didn't move. He didn't even look at her as she retreated back into the house. He simply sat there and let her leave.

He didn't waste anymore time and quickly returned the work that he had been doing. He would like to say that what she had said didn't bother him, but it did. It bothered him for reasons that he knew she could never understand. He was still standing by the log, where he had been sitting just a moment earlier enjoying his conversation, only now his mind was reeling from the words she had said. *Do my eyes look sad? What would a girl like that know about sadness, she has everything she could ever want.* Her question had lit a fire inside of him. All at once the numbness that he had been carrying with him for years was quickly being changed into anger. The soft lines of his face that normally carried a smile changed into the sharp edges of a scowl. His eyes narrowed and his fists began to clench. All of the emotion that he had carried silently inside of himself for years came roaring out onto his face. He had tried to be better than all of it but the truth was that he was angry. He became angry at his father for leaving him to be a man before he was ready. He was angry at his mother for running him off. He was mad at his brothers and sister for not helping to shoulder some of the burden, and he became mad at people like Kristen who had everything that they could ever want. Sweat began to bead up on his reddening face and he reached down and grabbed the axe up quickly, almost trying to squeeze through the handle with his grip. All of the pain and all of the sadness that he had known all of his life he had been able to hide. Suddenly, all it had taken was one harmless question from a girl that he barely knew to send all of his walls tumbling down.

Almost as if it would make it all go away, he turned to see the largest of the logs that he had cut sitting upright near the base of the tree. Raising the axe up high over his head, he swung down on it with all of his power. The axe blade came down, slicing through the air, and all the way down to the bottom of the log. The log seemed to explode from the power of his blow and he reached to grab another one. Swinging the axe even harder, the pieces went flying off like they had been hit with dynamite. He did this again and again. For what seemed to be forever he worked at a frenzied pace. With each blow of the axe he let out a cry as the blade crashed through the wood. With each blow he began to feel better and better. *My eyes look sad?* The calluses on his hands began to break and tear and the blood started to smear itself along the handle. He never slowed his pace. *What would she know about sadness?* He worked faster and faster, each time, letting out a yell as the axe came down to do its job. He realized why he had always worked so hard. When your body is bone tired, you don't have the energy to cry. With each cut he thought about the words that she had said, and the pain that he had known in his life. With each cut, the anger on his face seemed to lessen and the pain didn't feel so bad. His hands were throbbing from the blisters and his leg was aching from the cut near his knee. His arms and shoulders were swollen with blood from the rush of activity and they looked like they might pop. Each time he would stand the log up and send the two new halves flying to the side, only to grab another one and do it again. With one final blow of the axe, the anger on his face had gone away. Before he could catch his breath, and as if from somewhere deep inside of himself that he didn't know existed, a feeling came fighting up out of him stronger than he had ever felt before. He started to cry. The tears came rolling out of him and he couldn't make them stop. He didn't want them to stop. A steady stream was rolling down each cheek and the powerful young man broke down to one knee, bracing himself with the handle of his axe as he sobbed. It was the first time since the day that his father had left that he let himself cry. His body was shaking from fatigue and emotion and he was trying his best to catch his breath. The pain and the anger that he had been wearing on his face was dissolving away as if being washed away with each tear. He had been wishing so badly that he could let all of it go and as he crouched there on one knee covered in sawdust and sweat, he felt the load on his shoulders begin to ease and the pain in his heart begin to fade.

Why did she get to me? Why didn't I stop her? Almost at once he realized that this girl, this perfect stranger had let him feel something that he didn't know how to explain. He realized that even though it didn't make any sense, and even though he barely knew her, somehow she had let him feel again. He had never figured himself for the type of person that could ever feel something like that and as he kneeled there on the ground trying to regain his composure the pain that had taken over his face years ago slowly went away.

It was fifteen minutes before he was able to pull himself together and reach back for his axe. His hands were sore from the blisters on his palms but he didn't even seem to notice. He went back to work with a much less frenzied pace trying his best to make sense of everything that had just happened.

Looking out of the window of her bedroom, hidden in behind the curtains so that he could not see her, she had watched him as he had taken up his axe just moments before. Each blow that he let down had seemed so punishing. She could hear his muffled cries from inside her room. He had so much pain inside of him, and as she had watched him go down to a knee, she longed to be able to run out there to him. She had just stood there in the window and let him go. She knew she couldn't understand the loss and the loneliness that he knew, but she wished that he would let her get close enough to try. It didn't make sense to her why she felt for him the way she did. It was as if her heart had been asleep her entire life and it had woken up the day before when he walked in the door. She watched him as he broke down on the ground. She was surprised at how sad and weak he looked as he kneeled on the ground propped against the handle of his axe. He was normally so strong and powerful and she did her best to stay tucked in behind the curtains because she knew he wouldn't want her to see him. After a few minutes, he had picked himself back up and went back to splitting the logs as he had done before. She had never believed in this kind of thing before, but as she watched him go to work regaining his strong steady pace, she smiled to herself. He didn't come in on a great white horse, but maybe her knight in shining armor was meant to wear old faded blue jeans with a tear just below the knee.

NINE

The rocking chair had settled in to a much slower groan as Kristen rocked back and forth waiting on Jackson. Her watch said it was almost six o'clock and she began to wonder where he might be. It just wasn't like Jackson to be late and she was getting restless in the chair. Letting out a big yawn, her eyes were starting to feel heavy and the steady rocking and the breeze from up off of the lake that danced the wind chimes was making her sleepy. Everything was slowing down around her and the sun had started to set off in the distance. Her eyes were squinted as she looked down onto the water to see a few of the remaining boats that hadn't made it off the lake yet. Just through the trees at the bottom of the hill she could see the dock sitting out at the edge of the water.

With a large yawn she stared down at the dock and smiled to herself as her eyes began to feel heavy. Thinking back, she felt the years that had passed wash away till she was back on the dock four summers ago.

The days passed by quickly that summer for Kristen. If she would have known then that that summer out at the lake house would have been her last with Jackson for a long time, she might have found a way to slow down the clock. Two weeks had passed since Jackson had first come out to work for her dad; and she could feel the time she had with him slipping away. She had not spoken to

Jackson since the week before when they had had lunch together outside on the logs. He had been coming to work everyday as if nothing had been different and she managed to hide herself in the house while he was there. After hurting his feelings, all she wanted to do was talk to him but she couldn't think of what to say. He had finished all of his work with the trees that had been cut down a couple of days earlier. The previous morning her dad had set him up doing some work on the dock. She wanted to talk to him more than anything. She didn't know if he was mad at her, or if he wanted to talk to her at all.

Each morning she woke up to hear Jackson downstairs talking with her mom or dad and then he would be outside doing whatever job he needed to do that day. She would lay in the bed until she heard him go outside before venturing out downstairs to fix her breakfast. This routine had gone on for a week, and she could feel the knots forming in her stomach when she would hear him go outside. She longed to talk to him, but she couldn't find the words.

That morning she had heard him knock at the door, and she heard the muffled voices of Jackson and her mom talking in the kitchen. She was jealous of her mom for the time she was getting to spend with him and she wished that she could take her place. She heard a new voice added to the muffled tones from downstairs, meaning that her dad had come up from his workout to give Jackson his job for the day. Hearing the door close behind them, she threw the covers off and headed downstairs. Her mom was in the kitchen fixing some eggs and she could smell the fresh brewed coffee as she rounded the corner.

"Well good morning, sleepy head," her mom called out to her.

"Morning Momma," Kristen replied.

"Don't worry he has gone outside already," Sandy said.

When she said it, Kristen's face turned a glowing shade of red.

"Who?" she stammered back.

"Jackson; he has already gone outside for the day so you can come out of hiding."

"What are you talking about mom?" Kristen replied trying to have a sound of surprise in her voice.

"I know that you have been hiding from him for over a week now. It is not any coincidence that I don't see hide or hair of you in the morning until he is outside working for the day."

Kristen was still trying to hold the same look of shock on her face but she knew her mom could see right through it. "I don't know what you're talking about mom. I seriously have no idea what you are talking about."

"Ok, ok. You seem awful defensive to have no idea what I am talking about."

"Gah, momma, that's enough. I am going to take a shower."

Sandy smiled to herself as Kristen went back around the corner and up the stairs. She had notice that over the last week or so Jackson seemed to stay in the house talking a little longer than usual, and his looks towards the staircase leading up to the bedrooms had become frequent and obvious. She figured the attraction was harmless and she smiled as she thought about those same butterfly feelings that she had gotten so many years ago.

Ed and Jackson had made their way down to the dock where Jackson was going to be working that day. Ed had pointed out several things that needed to be done. Despite it being early in the morning, it was already showing signs of the hot day that was coming. The air was heavy and thick and sweat was beading up on both men's foreheads as they made their survey of the dock. Jackson was only a few inches taller than the doctor but his large arms and broad shoulders made him appear much larger. Despite being bigger, he still found himself intimidated by Ed. He watched quietly as his new boss pointed out what needed to be done.

"Ok buddy, these boards down here on the side need to be pulled up and replaced. They got busted up last winter and I haven't had a chance to fix them so you need to get those out of here," Ed explained. He pointed out the rips and tears in the boards. "When you get that done you will need to change the boards out over here by the boat. Do you know how to drive a boat?"

"No Sir," Jackson replied.

"Well then, when it gets time to change those boards out go get Kristen. She will need to back the boat out of the dock so that you can get to the boards to change them out."

"Yes sir." *I have to go get Kristen? Ah man. That is going to be awkward.*

"That should take you pretty much all day. I might be getting out of the hospital a little early today. You think you might be able to stick around and try some skiing?" he asked.

"I sure would love to, Doc, but I guess it will depend on what time I get done. I have to go watch my little brothers tonight so mom can go to work."

"Ok buddy, well I will try and get back soon so that we can go. Now be careful. Don't get hurt down here, and take your time and do it right," Dr. Taylor said. When he said it his tone was not a condescending one. It was fatherly as if meaning to do it right the first time so that they could go play.

While he listened, Jackson studied the doctor. He could see how fit he was. He was not a large man, but his back and chest seemed larger than they should have been for a man his size. His calf muscles popped out from his legs when he walked, a result of hundreds of miles of running. He could tell that the doctor was no stranger to a long work day, and it was because of that that Jackson didn't mind doing so many difficult jobs for him. He could see the sweat beading up on top of Ed's balding head and as he ran his hand across his forehead, it came away wet and sticky.

"Well buddy, I am gonna leave you to the heat. I have to go run and hop in the shower before I head up to the office so I better get going. Stick around this afternoon and we will try out a little skiing."

"Ok Doc, I am sure gonna try."

With that, the doctor turned on his heal and bounded up the hill towards the house. He moved with a quickness and agility not generally found in men his age. Jackson could see the muscles in his legs pumping as he made his way to the top of the hill and out of sight.

Jackson immediately turned his attention to the job at hand. It would take a couple of hours to get the old boards up and the new ones cut and put down before he would have to go get Kristen to move the boat. Maybe by then he would be able to think of something to say to her. The new boards that he would need had already been brought down to the dock. All Jackson needed were some tools to get the old boards up and a saw to cut the new ones to size. He made his way up to the garage and started his early morning routine of sorting through all of the clutter to find the things that he needed. Since he had been up there working for a couple of weeks, he had made great progress in organizing the garage into some sort of order so that he wouldn't have to waste hours hunting for the tools that he needed.

After finding everything that it would take to finish the job, he placed it all in a bucket and started back down the hill. He had been nervous in the garage almost afraid that Kristen may come out. He wanted to talk to her. He wanted to explain himself for the other day, but he wasn't sure what he could say without sounding desperate or pathetic. He had replayed the conversation a hundred times in his mind since then. Each time he would come to a part where she had told him a joke, he would catch himself smiling again and again.

He made his way out onto the dock after making it down the hill and laid out the tools that he had gathered in his bucket. The sun was already getting up and the heat was climbing with it. The breeze was not blowing at all and it made the air feel chewy and stagnant as he went about his work. Picking up a large crowbar from the dock he started working on pulling up the old damaged boards. Sweat was pouring down off of him, and even though it was still early in the day, the sun was beginning to go to work on his body.

Kristen had made her way out of the shower and into a bathing suit that she covered with a pair of shorts and a t-shirt. Her skin looked smooth and tanned as she slipped the light khaki shorts on and buttoned them up. She had pulled her hair back into a pony tail revealing the long slender lines of her face and neck. Tucking a free strand of hair behind her ear she turned from the mirror in her bedroom and headed downstairs. Reaching the bottom of the stairs she saw her mom and dad sitting in the kitchen.

"Hey Daddy, you aren't off to work yet?"

"I'm headed that way, just gonna go get in the shower real quick if you didn't use all my hot water."

"I left you a little bit," she smiled back, moving over to the kitchen. She began rummaging through the refrigerator to find something for breakfast.

She had her back to her parents when her dad said to her, "Kristen, I need you to do me a favor."

"Sure dad, what ya need?" she asked, still looking for some food.

"Jackson is working on the dock today and in a little while he is going to need you to come move the boat for him so he can finish his work. You think you could do that for me?"

When he said it Kristen froze. She knew that she had to say yes, because there was no way she was going to try and explain to her dad why she didn't want to.

"Yeah Daddy, it's not a problem." When she turned back to her dad she could see her mom standing next to him grinning from ear to ear. She had that all knowing look of a mother and Kristen's face turned blood red.

"Yeah, I am sure Kristen wouldn't mind helping one bit," Sandy said with her grin still beaming. As she said it, she looked right at Kristen. Ed stood there confused, not sure exactly what everybody was talking about.

"Well ok," her dad said, as he got out of his chair. "Just as long as you do it. I don't want him trying to get that boat out of there by himself. I need to get a shower." He shot toward the stairs still not sure why Sandy was still standing there grinning like a possum. *Maybe she has finally lost her mind,* he thought. He rounded the corner to head upstairs, as Kristen turned back towards the fridge and away from the knowing eyes of her mother.

"Not a word Mom, not a word."

"I didn't say a thing. I just know how much you love driving that boat. That's all I meant."

Yeah I bet, Kristen thought. She pulled out the orange juice and the eggs that she had wrestled from the back of the fridge.

"So what are you and Alyson doing today? Are you guys going to be around here, or are you gonna be gone today?"

"Well I have to go to into town in a little while to run some errands. Amanda Cooley is having her Bridal shower today so I am going to go to that about two o'clock. We should be back later on this afternoon. Why do you ask?"

"Oh no reason," Kristen replied. "Just thought I'd ask." She cracked the two eggs that she had taken from the carton onto the side of the large frying pan.

"Before you go down to the dock to help Jackson I want you to get your room cleaned up. It looks like a tornado blew through there."

"Oh it's not that bad, mom; you always exaggerate stuff."

"Not that bad? There are clothes in there that have been in the floor for six months. Not that bad. Girl, you better learn some domestic skills in a hurry. No man is ever gonna want to marry a woman that can't cook, and doesn't know how to do a load or two of her own laundry."

"Mom, I'm eighteen. Who cares if I know how to do my own laundry?"

"I bet Jackson cares."

When she said it, Kristen could feel the heat rising up from under her collar. Her mom was always saying stuff like that to get under her skin and it always worked. She wasn't even sure why her mom said it other than to see how many shades of red she could get to come out in Kristen's face.

"Mom. Seriously?"

"Ok, ok. I am going to get ready to go, but finish your breakfast and get your room clean."

"Ok, I will."

Sandy headed towards the stairs and disappeared to go change.

Gah, why does she say stuff like that, Kristen thought to herself. She had finished stirring the eggs, and reached up in the counter to pull down a plate. Pouring herself a large glass of orange juice, she threw the eggs onto a plate and took them up to her room so that she could enjoy her breakfast with a little peace and quiet.

After polishing off the last of her eggs, she started in on her room. It really did look bad and it took her about an hour to get down to the floor and get all of the clothes gathered and down to the laundry room. By the time she had finished, everyone in the house was gone. She thought that she had heard them say goodbye, but she was too busy thinking about what she might say to Jackson to respond. She was down in the laundry room throwing some of the dirty clothes into the washing machine when she heard the back door open.

TEN

"Kristen? You in here," Jackson called out.

"Yeah, I am in the laundry room. Be out in a minute."

"Ok, well I don't want to bother you. Your dad said you would move the boat for me so I could finish my work on the dock."

"Yeah, I will move it for you," she called out from the laundry room. "I will be down there in a minute."

"Ok," Jackson stammered back. "I will be down at the dock."

She heard the door close behind him and it took a few minutes for her heart to quit beating. She couldn't even see him when he came inside but the sound of his voice had made her flustered.

After getting all of her clothes put into the washing machine, she closed the lid and headed down to the dock to move the boat. As she moved down the dock, Jackson stopped what he was doing to look up. She looked amazing as she glided one foot in front of the other closer to him. Her pony tail bounced behind her and it took his breath away. He felt gross and ugly in his faded blue jeans and sweat soaked shirt. She looked so fresh and clean and her bright blue eyes seemed to glow as they caught the light from the sun.

The moment was tense. It was the first time they had been together since Jackson had gotten mad at her over a week ago, and neither of them knew what to say. Kristen did her best to keep the conversation strictly business.

"So you need the boat moved?" she asked not looking directly at him.

"Yeah, I need to get to those boards, and the boat is in the way."

"Ok, I can do that. I will just put it on the other side of the dock till you get done."

Jackson watched as she jumped in the boat and fired it up. She looked like she had done it a thousand times and quickly backed the boat out of its spot and moved it around the corner of the dock to the other side. Jackson had never been around boats growing up, so he was amazed at the power that he felt from the thunder of the engine and the ease in which she moved it all around. He wanted so badly to say something to her and his stomach was in knots trying to think of anything to say. He didn't think he could go another week without talking to her at all. The last few days had been miserable for him and he didn't want to wait anymore.

She pulled the boat around and tied it off to the other side. She never looked at him at all and as she hopped out of the boat, she moved towards the other end of the dock and back towards the hill leading up to the house. Jackson's heart was racing and he didn't know what to do. He didn't want her to leave.

"They aren't always sad," he said quietly.

She stopped walking and turned slowly back to him. "What?" she asked.

"My eyes, they aren't always sad," he said again.

"Jackson I didn't mean to . . ."

"It's ok," he interrupted. His heart was racing and he didn't know what to say. He stood up from where he had been crouched down working on the dock, and they stood there on opposite ends staring right into each others eyes.

"You were right. I guess my eyes have been sad for so long that I forgot about it. I don't think I have ever even given it much thought until you said something last week."

"I shouldn't have said anything. I'm sorry. I really am sorry. I had no right to dig like that. You remember me telling you that I don't always bring my brain into things like this? Well now you know it's true."

He smiled. He had needed to hear her voice so badly despite how awkward the conversation had become.

She was still several feet away so she took a step closer to him. Moving in closer from her side of the dock, he could feel his heart begin to beat faster and faster.

"I am sorry for getting mad at you," he said looking down at the dock. "I had no right to get mad at you. I don't know why I got so mad. I guess I just thought I was a little better at hiding all of this stuff than I really am."

"Jackson, you don't have to hide what you're going through," she said, still moving slowly towards him. "You don't have to feel ashamed. So what your dad left, so what your brothers and sister aren't helping you. You are doing the best you can. You shouldn't be ashamed of all of that other stuff. You can't help it."

"You don't understand."

"No, your right; I haven't gone through all of that stuff, but I know what sadness feels like. Don't look at all of this stuff sitting around and think that this is some kind of happiness, Jackson. Having this stuff doesn't make you happy. I am still lonely and I am still bored, and restless, and I think I feel sad everyday," she said still moving closer to him. She was only a few feet away now and he could smell her perfume as the wind picked up from the lake and whirled the scent all around him.

"So how does it get better, how do you make it get better?" he asked with a look of desperation in his eyes.

She took one more step toward him but before she could answer her foot caught on one of the boards that he had started to pull up on the floor of the dock and she felt herself falling over into the water. It happened in an instant and she closed her eyes preparing for the contact with the water. She threw her arms out in front of her as she flew toward the lake. She was about to hit the water when she felt an iron strong grip wrap itself around her shirt and in one fluid motion pull her back up. She opened her eyes in a daze to find herself wrapped up in his arms. She could see Jackson smiling down at her. She was flustered and out of breath and her heart was racing. She could feel the strength and power of his arms and she felt small wrapped up inside of them.

She whispered to him, "It gets better by having someone to catch you when you fall."

When she said it, she could feel Jackson pull her in closer. Her body felt electric as he leaned in closer to her. Her heart was racing and she could feel his heart pounding in his chest. Leaning in closer, he could feel her breath on his cheek and he could feel his arms trembling with anticipation. He had never felt anything like this before and he wasn't sure what to do. He leaned in a little closer and felt his eyes close. As he leaned in closer and his lips began to tremble he heard a voice call out to him.

"Hey guys, what's going on?"

Jackson jerked up when he heard Ed's voice come from the other side of the dock and he jumped back away from Kristen. As he stepped away from her, still shocked to see her dad home so soon, his foot caught on the half exposed board and he went reeling out into the water.

He came back up from underneath the water gasping for air and shocked at the chill of the lake water. He looked up to see Ed and Kristen looking down at him both doing their best not to laugh. Wiping his face and doing his best to tread water with his work boots and blue jeans on, he swam back over to the edge of the dock to see Ed's hand extended out to him. He reached up and grabbed his hand as Ed struggled to pull the water logged young man up out of the lake.

"Daddy, what are you doing home?" Kristen asked.

"Well I got through with work and thought I would come and give Jack a hand. Seems like you were already down here helping him," Ed replied looking at Kristen.

"Oh, Jackson caught me. I moved the boat like you asked and when I came over here to see what he was doing, I tripped on that board. Jackson caught me from going in the water."

"Yeah, looks like he caught you pretty good," Ed said as he made the last pull to get Jackson all the way back on the dock.

"Yeah, she fell, Doc. I was just trying to keep her from falling in."

"Well maybe somebody should have caught you," he said smiling at the soaked teenager.

Jackson stood up from the dock and did his best to ring out his shirt as water dripped all over the dock.

"Well, I don't guess you have a change of clothes with you," Ed said, smiling at Jackson.

"No Sir."

"Well I know I don't have any shirts that will fit you, but I have a pair of shorts that should work. Lets go up to the house and get you into some dry clothes."

Jackson hoped by his reaction that this meant that the doctor was not mad at him. He had a tough time getting a read on Ed and he was embarrassed that he had been caught in such a compromising position. The last thing he wanted was to do something to lose this job. The thought of not being able to come out and see her anymore was more horrible than he could stand. He was even more upset that he hadn't gotten a chance to get that kiss from Kristen.

ELEVEN

The three of them walked back up to the house from the dock. Jackson walked a couple of steps behind Kristen and her dad not wanting to do anything that might make him mad or that might prompt him to ask Jackson to leave. This job had become more than just a paycheck to him. He knew that this would be his only way of spending time with Kristen and he knew that all of that hung on Ed's decision.

They got back up to the house and Jackson waited on the back porch for Ed to bring down some shorts for him to wear. Kristen waited out on the porch next to Jackson as her dad went inside.

"Sorry bout you falling in the lake," she said with a smile.

"Yeah, I guess that whole catch you when you fall thing only works if you are strong enough," he said smiling back.

"Yeah, and it has a lot to do with not getting caught kissing on the dock by your dad."

When she said it, they both laughed. It was not exactly the ending that either of them had been hoping for, but it had still felt incredible. Her mind was spinning from the thought of being in his arms. She wished so badly that she could fall off of something else so that he could catch her. She was amazed at how quickly he had moved to catch her and how strong he was to pull her back up.

"Well, at least one of us is dry," she said. "I guess those muscle of yours aren't just for splitting logs." When she said it, his face turned bright red.

Before he could come up with a response Ed came back outside holding a pair of shorts.

"Ok buddy, here you go. These should fit. Just use that downstairs bathroom and get changed and we will work on getting those boards up where the boat was."

"Yes Sir, sounds good." Jackson took the shorts and headed back inside the house leaving Ed out on the porch with Kristen.

They both stood there not saying anything for a minute or two when her dad finally broke the silence.

"Guess you need to watch your step out on that dock," he said looking down at the lake.

"Daddy, it was nothing, it was, well I fell, and the board, and then Jackson's arms, I mean."

Ed laughed. "I'm just messing with you," he said turning back to her. "Just remember, you are leaving in the fall. Just be careful that you don't add one more goodbye you will have to say when its time to leave home." When he said it, he walked down off the porch and back down towards the dock.

She wasn't exactly sure how to take what he just said, but she didn't have time to think about it long. Jackson came out of the door behind her. He looked much more casual than he normally did. In his bare feet and shorts instead of his usual jeans it made him seem less old and more playful. He wasn't wearing a shirt, and she noticed the necklace that was normally tucked in behind his shirt hanging in the middle of his chest.

"Nice shorts," she said as they turned towards the steps to head down towards the dock.

"Yeah thanks," he said sarcastically. "Shorts really aren't my style but wet blue jeans aren't either."

"So, that necklace you have on. What is it? I notice that you never take it off."

"Oh yeah this? I have had it on so long that I forget that it's on here," he said grabbing the small medallion that hung down from a silver chain. "It was my grandfather's. He gave it to me before he died. I was just a boy. He had it for years and it meant the world to him. I used to climb into his lap and look at it when I was a boy," Jackson said as they walked slowly down the hill to the dock. "He got drafted and was getting ready to leave for the war. He had been dating my grandmother for a long time but he said he couldn't marry her yet. He told her he had some things he needed to take care of and when he got back he would marry her. This necklace that he had had since he was a boy, he gave it to her. He told her he would come back to get it, and when he did he would marry her."

"Some things to take care of?" she asked, looking over at him to admire the necklace.

"Yeah, some things to take care of. It was his way of saying that he had some stuff to go do that she wouldn't understand but he promised he would come back when he got it all done."

"So I take it he made it back," Kristen said.

"Married fifty-three years before she passed away," he replied. "He died a couple of years later. I think he died out of sadness more than anything."

"What a sweet story."

"Yeah, my grandfather could really get those nurses at the nursing home worked up with that one. He really was good at telling those stories."

They had made it down to the dock to see Ed already down there. He was working on the crowbar trying to pull off some of the boards that Jackson hadn't gotten to yet.

"Hey Doc, I got that," Jackson shouted as they came into sight.

"Oh no, it's okay, buddy, Just go ahead and start cutting the new boards to go in. That way we can get done with this," Ed replied in a strained voice as he tugged at the boards.

"Ok. I have the saw set up already so it shouldn't take too long."

The sun had moved to the far side of the sky but the mid afternoon heat was still working on all three of them as they worked on the dock. Jackson was cutting the new boards to go in place and Ed worked to free the damaged boards from the floor of the dock. Kristen had taken a seat in the boat and propped her feet up watching the two of them work. Ed would call out the measurements and Jackson would quickly measure the boards and make the cut. Kristen watched as the two of them worked together. Whether or not either of them realized it, she saw several similarities in the two men. The work that they did had struck some kind of harmony and the words that they spoke were few, and intermittent. It was as if they anticipated the others next move and without having to say anything they would already be moving to the next thing that needed to be done. Jackson was working and sweating all over and Kristen watched as the muscles of his chest and stomach relaxed and constricted as he worked. The necklace that he wore around his neck would hang freely in the air as he bent over to make a cut only to fall back into place in the middle of his chest when he would right himself.

Watching his arms work, she couldn't help but long to be back in them again. He was so powerful and yet when he held her he possessed a balance of strength and tenderness. It was the tenderness that she enjoyed most, but it was his strength that had made her feel so small and safe. An hour passed and the work was nearing completion. Jackson had bent down to hand Ed the last board when the cut just below his knee started to bleed. All of the activity of the day had aggravated the injury, and the blood began to roll down his calf and onto the dock. Ed caught the trickle of blood running down Jackson's leg out of the corner of his eye.

"What did you do to your leg?" he asked. His tone was less concerned and more inquisitive.

"Oh this? Nothing, it's nothing."

"No, what is it? Did you do that here? Let me look at that."

He moved over to Jackson to examine the cut on his knee. Jackson was nervous and Kristen had sprung up from her relaxed position on the boat. Ed looked at the large cut on his leg as Jackson and Kristen shot scared looks at each other. They both knew that if he found out that the cut had happened out here, and if he found out that he did it with the chainsaw and everyone in his family knew about it, Jackson would be on the fast track to unemployment. Ed was not an unkind man but he had little time for stupid mistakes, or, more importantly, deception.

"Did you do that out here?" he asked again.

"Well I," but before he could answer Kristen interrupted.

"Jackson, did you cut your leg when you dove out to catch me?"

Jackson looked at her confused, not knowing what to say, and Ed looked at them both trying to figure out what was going on.

"Um, yeah I guess I didn't notice it earlier. All the commotion and everything. I must have hit my leg on the dock when I dove out to get you."

"You did this on the dock?" Ed asked not truly buying the story.

"Yeah, he did it on the dock, daddy," Kristen said climbing out of the boat and over to her father. Putting her arms around her father, she said, "He did it to save me, Daddy."

"You sure you did this on the dock today?" Ed asked again.

"Daddy, of course he did, now come on, Jackson, we have to get you up to the house and get that cleaned up. No telling what kind of germs you have in that thing."

"Well ok," Ed said, softening at the embrace of his little girl. "I was just checking. If you say so darling. You two get up to the house and get that cleaned up. I am gonna put this last board down."

"Thank you, Daddy; we will be back in a minute."

Jackson just stood there dazed, as if he had forgotten how to speak. He didn't want to say something stupid. He was amazed at how she had melted her father so quickly. If she had that kind of power over her dad it scared him to think what she could do to him.

"Come on, Jackson, let's get you cleaned up," she said pulling at his arm.

Neither of them spoke until they were well out of earshot of the dock.

"Wow, how did you do that?" Jackson asked. "I thought I was on my way out of here. I couldn't think of what to say, and he was just looking at me. Do you think that he really bought it?"

"Doesn't matter," she laughed. "I said it, and he wouldn't want to make his little girl mad. He won't ever say anything else about it."

"Well, I owe you one."

"Yeah you do," she smiled back at him.

They made it up to the house and walked into the kitchen. Kristen sat Jackson down at the kitchen table and went to the pantry to get some more of the bandages that her mom had gotten for him the week before. She came back into the kitchen where she had left him sitting when her mom came around the corner.

"Hey, what are you two doing?" her mom asked. "Jackson, did you cut your leg again?"

"Mom, he cut his leg on the dock," Kristen said.

"No, he didn't he cut his leg on the—" but before she could finish, Kristen cut her a look and at once her mom was up to speed. "Oh, he cut his leg on the dock, huh?"

"Yeah, he cut his leg on the dock to save me from going in the water and if dad asks that is exactly what happened."

"Hey, your secret is safe with me," Sandy said. "I don't want your father flipping out and doing something dumb. More stuff has gotten done in the two weeks that Jackson has been here then in the last two years. I ain't gonna mess that up."

While she was talked, Kristen cleaned the cut and wrapped it in a bandage. She was scared that her father was going to flip out, and she was thankful to have avoided the entire mess.

"Ok, it's all good to go," she said. "I didn't wrap it too tight, did I?"

"No, it's perfect," Jackson replied.

As he said it, Ed came in the back door soaked in sweat.

"Well the last board is on. If you two don't mind, could you get all of the tools and stuff up from the dock? I would really appreciate it. How's your leg, Jack?" he asked with a littler more concern than he had had earlier.

"Oh it's good as new, Doc. Kristen got it all wrapped up for me. I'm gonna run down and get that stuff up." Jackson was anxious to get out of the kitchen and had no desire to answer any more questions.

"I'll go with you," Kristen rang out, as they both shot towards the door.

TWELVE

The sun was beginning to get down low in the sky and the clock on the dash told Jackson that he was really late. He was a little upset at himself for being late but he knew she would understand. He had made a good living over the last few years by always being on time and working as hard as he could. He hoped that she would cut him a little slack if he was a little late this one time. The oncoming cars had turned on their headlights and so each one that passed looked like a streak of light as he sped down the winding lake road. He looked down on the seat next to him to see the letter that he had written. He reached down to pick it up in time to see a wave of light come pouring over the car. As was always the case, his thoughts were of Kristen.

They went out onto the back porch and down towards the dock. They smiled at each other as they got away from the house like they had just gotten away with something. The sun was working down in the sky on the far side of the lake and the air was starting to cool.

They moved around the dock to pick up all of the tools. They worked while they talked casually about nothing at all. As one would pass by the other to place another tool in the basket, they would brush up against the other. It was a purely intentional move meant to seem accidental. They danced around each other on the dock, gently touching each other, with one never really looking at the other. They went on this way for half an hour. Jackson picked up the large basket of tools and they walked together back up the hill. Neither of them was sure what was happening between them. It was something that they had never felt before and they felt excited to be next to each other. Placing the tool basket down in the garage Jackson turned to Kristen.

"Well I guess that's it," he said. "I should probably be getting home." He looked up from the ground to see her reaction. The look on her face spoke of disappointment. She wasn't ready for him to go.

"Do you have to go already? Shouldn't we go back down to the dock and make sure we got up all of the tools?"

"Well I am pretty sure we got all the tools," he said in a matter of fact sort of way.

She rolled her eyes at him for not understanding what she meant and she shot him a glance, the same one that she had given her father earlier.

"Oh, well maybe we could go back down there and take one last look," he said with a smile.

"Yeah, plus we need to put the boat back."

"Oh yeah, I almost forgot about putting the boat back," he replied.

He turned to head back towards the dock and noticed that Kristen was not beside him. He looked back to see her poking her head inside the door to say something to her mom. He couldn't hear what was said but she came skipping back out to him and they walked back down to the dock.

"What was that all about," he asked.

"What?"

"I mean what did you just say to your mom?"

"Oh I told her that we would be back in a little bit."

"Back in a little bit? Are you kidnapping me?"

"Maybe, so shut up and do what you're told," she said laughing her playful maniacal laugh.

"Yes ma'am."

They got down to the dock and Kristen jumped in the boat and fired it up. Jackson stood on the dock watching her. Every move she made seemed so graceful to him and he shifted back on his heels with his hands plunged deep in his pockets trying not to stare too long.

She looked back at him, and yelled over the engine, "Well are you coming or not?"

"On there?"

"Yeah, on here; let's go, boy, I ain't got all day."

He moved quickly over to her and jumped into the boat. Within a minute they were out of the little cove and out onto the main body of the lake. The air felt cool on his body, and the evening was perfect. He caught himself staring at her. She had taken down her ponytail, and her long brown hair whipped around behind her. The sun was working down to twilight and all he could think to himself was how beautiful she was.

"Too fast for you?" she yelled out over the sound of the wind and the engine.

"Is this all you got?" he yelled back with a smile.

At his response, she cut the wheel hard and the back end of the boat went sliding around behind them on the water. Jackson's mouth dropped open and she laughed at the expression on his face. They sped across the water towards the other end of the lake.

"Very funny," he yelled.

As he was getting ready to yell something else to her, everything got really quiet. She pulled back on the throttle and the wind, and the roar of the boat motor all went away. Jackson's hair was standing up everywhere from the wind and she laughed as she turned to him switching off the key.

"So you are gonna kidnap me," he said. "I'm not jumping, and I wouldn't be worth much for a ransom."

She laughed, "Don't worry; I am not going to make you jump. Look," as she said it she pointed back up to the sun that had worked its way down to the tree tops on the far side of the sky.

"Wow, it's beautiful," he said, looking out at the setting sun.

"Yeah it is," she said looking only at Jackson.

When she said it, he looked back at her and their eyes locked for what felt like minutes.

"Thanks for today," he said to break the silence. A lump was beginning to form in his throat. "You kind of saved me from your dad."

"Hey, it's the least I could do after you cut your leg open on the dock to save me from going in."

When she said it they both laughed.

She dropped the anchor and moved to the large bench style seat on the back of the boat. She gave Jackson a look signaling him to come sit next to her. He moved nervously over to her and sat down on the bench. He was scared at being this close to her and he wasn't sure what to do. He was glad that she had brought him out here with her. Despite how nervous he was to be alone with her on the boat, he felt a comfort around her that he couldn't explain.

Her smell was intoxicating, and he thought she was a thousand times more beautiful than any sunset. His heart was beating out of his chest, and he could tell that she was nervous, too.

"So you bring a lot of guys out here?" he said with a smile.

"As a matter of fact, Mr. Bryce, I have brought hundreds." She smiled at him as she said it.

The air was getting cooler and the sun was sinking lower as Jackson shyly reached his arm around her. When she felt his arm go around her shoulders, a chill went up her body. She knew she had never felt anything like it. He pulled her in close and she laid her head on his shoulder to watch the sun sink.

"Jackson."

"Yeah," he replied.

"I'm sorry about last week. I didn't mean to make you mad."

"It's ok; it was more what was going on in my head than what you said to me."

"Yeah maybe, but I shouldn't have said it." Pausing for a minute she added, "If I were to ask you the same question again would you get mad at me?"

"I think you kind of just asked me."

"Well then, why do your eyes look so sad?" she asked, lifting up her head to look at him.

"I am not sure you could understand, Kris," he said.

"Try me."

"It's just that I am eighteen years old, and I am scared that this is as good as it is ever going to be for me. I have to take care of my brothers, I have to basically support my mom, and the one girl that I have ever truly liked in my life is going to leave in a couple of months. It's just that, I feel like I got cheated. Ya know? I feel like I didn't get a fair break."

She looked at him trying to understand the words. "I know it has to feel that way but you can beat it. You can be whatever you want to be. I know you. I have seen how hard you work. Why couldn't you go be something great?"

"People like me don't get to be great, Kristen. People like me will always work for people like you. It's classic, isn't it? The haves and the have-nots."

"Jackson, I never figured you for a pessimist."

"I am not being pessimistic; I am being real. I am not lying to myself pretending like I am gonna get the same shot at this life as you are, or anybody else for that matter."

"Jackson, so what?" she said, getting frustrated. "Everybody comes to two points, Jackson. The first is when you decide what it is you want out of this life, and the second is when you decide if you are willing to do what it takes to get there. If you want something in this life you have got to go get it."

"I am not trying to sound mean, but what would you know about it?" he asked.

"Do you think my father has always had all of this? Do you think he just woke up one day and somebody handed him all of this? No. He worked for everything that he has. He came from nothing. His family was a lot more poor than your family is, but he decided to find a way. I may not have gone through it but I know what it takes to struggle, because I have seen my father working his tail off my whole life so I wouldn't have to. Now maybe it isn't fair. Maybe you should have been given more Jackson. Maybe you didn't get a good shot to go get what you want, but you have to figure out a way to do it anyway."

She went on for a few minutes as Jackson sat and listened to the words that she was saying. She was right. He had been figuring out excuses for why he wasn't going to make it for so long that he forgot that he still had some choices.

"So what happens now?" he asked.

"What do you mean," she replied back to him.

"I mean, where do I go from here?"

"Well, the first thing you have to do is figure out what you want, and then figure out what it will take to make it happen."

At that moment, Jackson knew what he wanted. He knew with absolute certainty that he wanted her. He had to have her, but he knew that a girl like that could never be with a guy like him. He had to make some changes. He had to get a plan. For the first time since he was a little boy he felt like it was ok for him to have dreams again. He knew that what he wanted more than anything else in the world was her. At that moment, he knew that everything he did from there on out was to somehow find a way to deserve this girl.

"I think I know what I want," he said. "I think I know." As he said it, he stared deep into her eyes. She felt like he could see all the way into her soul and the amazing thing about it all is she didn't want to stop him. She had never felt like this before and curled up next to him there on the boat she felt safe and happy.

"Kristen?"

"Yeah," she responded.

"Do you still think there is no such thing as a prince charming, or a knight in shining armor?" he asked, looking out at the sun that had almost completely set.

With her head on his shoulder and her hand on his chest she replied, "I wasn't sure for a long time, in fact I was pretty sure that there wasn't one at all."

"Oh," he replied looking down at the ground disappointed in her answer, "So what do you think now?"

"Well, I have a question for you."

"Ok," he answered.

"Can prince charming wear blue jeans?"

When she said it, he smiled at her in one of his smiles that covered his face from ear to ear. "Yeah, I think he can."

When he said it, he reached his hand out and put it on the side of her cheek. He pulled her up close to him, and he knew she must be able to feel his heart pounding beneath his chest. He pulled her closer and closer until he could feel her breath on his lips. Closing his eyes, he leaned in the rest of the way, and their lips met as the sun disappeared behind them.

When their lips met, his body came alive and his head was reeling. He had never felt anything like it before. She uncurled herself from sitting next to him and brought herself up on top of him. They kissed as if they would never be able to do it again. They wrapped themselves up in each others bodies and neither of them had ever felt so alive. His arms felt so strong and yet, as he pulled her close to him, they handled her like delicate glass. She felt so safe with him and she craved his touch.

They laid there together for what must have been a half hour but it only felt like seconds to either one of them. The sun had set and the few wisps of light that were left were slowly going away for the night.

Jackson grabbed her wrist to look at her watch, "We should go."

"Yeah, I guess we should. I don't know if the lights work on this boat and my dad would kill me if I got in trouble out here. Plus, I don't want you to be late."

"Don't you worry about me, and all you would have to do is give your Dad that puppy dog look you do and he would melt."

Kristen laughed as she sat up from the seat and moved over to start the boat. "Yeah, the puppy dog look gets him every time."

As the boat cranked up underneath her and she idled the boat around to point it back home, Jackson slipped up behind her and kissed her on the cheek.

"Thanks for tonight. I don't really stop for many sunsets," he said.

"Well now when you see one remember me." His kiss sent a chill down her back and she could feel his body pressed up against hers. She didn't want to leave.

"You better sit down. I would hate to lose you off the side of the boat out here in the dark," she said with a smile.

Climbing back down in the seat next to her, Jackson stared out onto the lake that was being covered in darkness. All around the shoreline lights dotted here and there signaling a dock, a boat, or a house. As the roar of the boat drowned everything out, Jackson's mind was swimming. He knew without a doubt as the sun disappeared for the night and the air cooled itself around him that he had felt something tonight he had never truly known before. As they rounded the corner back to the dock, he could think of only one thing. For the first time in his life Jackson was in love.

THIRTEEN

The next morning when Jackson pulled up in front of the house he didn't look like the same person that had pulled up the morning before. His feet hit much more softly on the driveway as he made his way to the door. He did not have the look of someone who had come to work. In fact, for the first time in his life, he had the look of someone who didn't have a care in the world. He knocked on the front door as he had been doing for the last couple of weeks but this time he was surprised when it opened. Kristen was standing there dressed, with a fresh cup of hot coffee in her hands.

"Wow, hey, I wasn't expecting you to come to the door this morning. Are you sick or something? What are you doing out of bed?" Jackson asked in a teasing voice.

"Oh, I just thought you might like a cup of coffee," she replied extending the cup out to him.

"That's for me? You don't want it?"

"Oh no, I can't stand the way it tastes, but I thought you might like it. Come on in," she said as he took the cup from her. "Dad should be up in a minute; he is downstairs working out."

"Ok, good deal. So does breakfast come with the coffee?" he asked winking at her.

"Don't push your luck, Bryce. At least you got some coffee."

They moved over to the table in the kitchen to wait for her dad to finish his workout. It was strange for Jackson to see Kristen up so early. Apparently the night before had gotten to her, too. Seated facing each other, Jackson took a big sip of the coffee she had made. He did his best to hide his expression as he choked down the motor oil looking coffee. It tasted horrible but he did his best to hide his expression.

"So how is it?" She asked with a look anxiety on her face.

"Perfect," he replied smiling back at her. "It is perfect." When he said it, he left his eyes locked on her, and she did nothing to hide her smile.

"It's gonna be hot today," he said trying to get the taste of the coffee out of his mouth.

"Yeah I don't know if I am going to be able to just sit there and watch you work all day with this kind of heat," Kristen replied slyly.

He smiled when she said it. He didn't need the help, but he appreciated the company more than she knew.

"So, any idea what your Dad has planned for me today?"

"I don't have a clue," she said looking out of the window overlooking the lake. "Whatever it is I am pretty sure it won't be fun."

They talked for a few more minutes and like all of their conversations, it never seemed long enough. Jackson had been there for about fifteen minutes when Ed came up through the door.

"Well hey, buddy, you been waiting here long?"

"Oh no, sir, just a few minutes. I bet I haven't been sitting here ten minutes."

"Oh, well, that's good. Kristen, what's got you up so early this morning?" he asked looking at Jackson and not at Kristen.

"Oh I don't know, Dad, just couldn't sleep so I figured I might as well get on up out of bed."

"Well wonders never cease. I guess there is a first time for everything," he said moving over towards the coffee pot.

She didn't pay any attention to her dad and watched Jackson as he took another big sip of her coffee. It made her smile to see him drinking it. Ed poured a cup of the coffee that she had made, and walked around the counter to the kitchen table where they had been sitting. He blew on the steaming cup and then took a large slurping sip, freezing the moment the coffee hit his lips. The coffee was strong and thick and his mouth was full of coffee grounds.

"Oh my god, what happened to the coffee?" he asked walking back over to the sink to pour it out. He coughed as he tried to clean his mouth of the foul taste.

"What's wrong with it, Daddy? You don't like it," she asked turning from her father to look at Jackson.

"Darling, this is the worst cup of coffee ever made. Did you put a filter in it?" Ed reached over to the coffee pot to inspect the damage.

"I don't know, Daddy. I wasn't sure how to make it. Is it not any good?" She was looking at Jackson trying to get a read on his expression.

"It would have been good if you would have put a filter in it," he said still coughing from the bad taste in his mouth.

The expression on Jackson's face looked like a child who had gotten his hand caught in the cookie jar. His eyes were as big as saucers, and he was trying to hide his face behind the cup she had given him.

"So it's not any good, huh?" she asked flashing a sly grin to Jackson.

Ed was still on the other side of the kitchen trying to wipe the coffee grounds out of his mouth. "Baby, I am not trying to hurt your feelings, but I think you better leave the coffee making to somebody else. Jackson, are you drinking this stuff?" Jackson didn't move and the look showed that he knew he had been caught.

"It's not too bad," he whispered to her hoping that Ed wouldn't hear.

"Not too bad? Boy, you need to go get checked out if you don't think that is a bad cup of coffee. Give that cup to me and I will make us another pot." As he said it, he moved over to Jackson to take the mug. Ed reached down for the mug in time for Jackson to look back at Kristen and take one last sip.

She smiled to herself while she watched him try and choke down the bad cup of coffee. She hoped he would always care for her enough to drink her bad coffee.

The next few weeks felt like a fairy tale to Kristen. Where she used to sleep in, staying in the bed for hours past daylight, she found herself up at dawn waiting on Jackson to pull up in front of the house in his beat up old pickup. The feeling of butterflies she got in her stomach felt stronger to her each day that she would watch him stroll down the driveway. She noticed a lightness in his footsteps, too. He had a different look about him and she liked the change. From the moment that he pulled up in front of the house until he left that evening he seemed to have a smile beamed across his face.

It had been almost a week since the two of them had taken the boat out onto the lake but for the two of them it felt like only a moment. When Jackson would reach the house, Kristen would meet him at the door to steal a kiss before anyone knew he was there. He would get his new assignment from her father or would go to work immediately to finish whatever task he had started the day before.

"What's he got you working on today?" Kristen asked as he made his way into the familiar house.

"I don't know," he replied. "Probably going to do a little work on the car today. I think its 'bout time to change the oil." He was smiling at her as he said it. His face looked younger and he had begun to lose all trace of the serious scowl that he used to carry around.

"Well that doesn't sound too bad," she said back to him. "At least you don't have to use that chainsaw today," she said with a smile. While she spoke she retreated from the door where she had met him and headed back in to the house and towards the kitchen waving at him to follow.

"You get a real kick out of reminding me of that don't you? You ever gonna let me forget about it?"

"Not if I can help it," she answered back with a devilish grin.

Before he could respond, Ed rounded the corner of the staircase that led to his upstairs bedroom.

"Hey Buddy," Ed called out to him.

"Morning Doc."

"You ready to do a little work?" When he said it he shot a look over at Kristen. He was still trying to figure out exactly what was going on. He had not seen his daughter out of bed that early before and he knew she wasn't up for the morning air.

"Hey, you know me, Doc. Let's get to work."

"Well I need you to change the oil in the car today. You think you could do that?"

"Oh, yes sir, no problem," Jackson replied as he fixed himself a cup of coffee. He was feeling more and more at home and no longer waited for anyone to ask him if he needed anything. He also didn't want to have to wait for Kristen to make him a cup, since she had proven that she wasn't very good at it. "Do you have all of the stuff here that I will need?" he asked.

"Yeah, everything you need should be in the garage," Ed replied. "If you are missing anything that you need feel free to run down to the store and pick it up and I will pay you back."

"Ok, sounds good. I think I am going to go ahead and get a jump on it so I can beat some the heat. You gonna be around today, Doc?"

"No, I am heading towards the hospital in just a couple of minutes. Sandy will be here for a little while, but I think she is taking Alyson to some kind of pool party so I don't think that they will be around for too long. So it looks like it is just you two here today. If she starts to get on your nerves just send her to her room," he said smiling at his daughter, "That's what I do."

Jackson laughed, "Ok Doc, I will definitely keep that in mind."

Kristen shot them both a look that sent them in to a giant laugh. "Alright, enough of that you two. Jackson, don't you need to get to work?" When she said it she gave him a quick jab to the arm.

"Yeah, I better get to work," he said laughing a little and rubbing his arm as if the jab had hurt him. "No need to get violent."

She shot a smile back to him and followed him out into the garage. Together they found everything that he would need to finish the job and he slid down onto his back to scoot underneath the car. It was already starting to get warm outside and she watched as the sweat began to bead up on his arms. He fumbled around underneath the car for a minute or two before he poked his head out from underneath.

"Well are you just gonna stand there or are you going to give me a hand?"

"Who me?" she asked in a surprised voice. "I don't know the first thing about changing oil."

"Well today is the day you are going to learn," he replied with a grin.

"I don't know, Jack, it doesn't sound like much fun; and what about my nails," she said beginning to strut around the garage like some kind of movie star. In a strong southern belle type drawl she said, "What would I do if I damaged my manicure?"

He laughed at her strutting around and took a swipe at her leg as she came near him. "Come on, Scarlet, time to get those hands dirty."

"Ok, I'm coming." She crawled down on her back and slid down next to him under the car. "Is this your idea of a good time? Getting the girl of your dreams to do all of your dirty work for you?" When she said it, she laughed but the look on his face was more serious.

"I think you are the girl of my dreams. I don't think I have ever quite felt like this before." As he spoke she could feel the heat from his breath and the warmth of his body and it sent chills running down her spine. She was still not quit used to being this close to him and her heart was racing and she could feel his beating just as fast. The tension felt extreme. They had both turned towards each other just slightly and their lips were moving closer and closer.

In a whisper she spoke to him, "I bet you pull this trick with all the girls."

"Yeah," he smiled, "The old pretending like you are going to change the oil so you can make your move routine. I bet I have used it a hundred times." They moved closer but before their lips could touch Jackson felt a bead of what felt like sweat running down his cheek. Moving his hand to his face they both fell in to laughter as he wiped the drops of oil away.

"Wow, that was perfect timing," she said. "I thought you were about to make a move on me." She was laughing all the way from her belly now.

"Oh, you think that's funny, do you?" He took a smear of the oil that he had gotten on his face and wiped it across her cheek. When he did it, she let out a scream and they wrestled around underneath the car trying to smear each other with the oil. He grabbed her wrist and pulled her in close and leaned in again to give her a kiss. As their lips were beginning to meet, he heard a throat being cleared. They both looked down at their feet that were sticking out from underneath the car to see Ed standing over them.

"What's going on you two?" he asked in a tone that was not harsh or mean but that definitely demanded an answer.

"Oh, he was teaching me how to change the oil on the car, Daddy," Kristen yelled out from underneath the car. She was glad that he couldn't see her face.

"Well let's just make sure that that is what we are getting done. I have to go to work; I will see you two later."

Jackson held his breath for what seemed like ten minutes until he heard her father crank up his other car and head out of the driveway. All at once he let his air out and they both started laughing.

"All right, let's get this thing done. That was embarrassing," he said. He could feel how red his face was and he was glad he had not had to look at the doctor. With his eyes closed, trying to regain his composure, a smile crept across his face as he felt an oil covered finger run all the way down the bridge of his nose.

FOURTEEN

With the first task of the morning completed, Jackson and Kristen spent the rest of the day working on the different odds and ends that he had not been able to get to over the last couple of weeks. It was blistering hot outside but the tasks were easy and the company was a welcome addition to the day. He had come to love every minute that he spent with Kristen and so he never thought much about the work.

Jackson was wiping his hands with a rag while Kristen scanned down a piece of paper that he had given her that morning.

"Alright partner, what's next on the list?" he asked as he patted her on the back like she was an old football buddy.

"Don't know. Guess it depends on what you feel like doing," she answered back with a cough from the lick he gave her on the back. "Whatever it is you're on your own cause I don't know how to do any of it."

"What do you mean you don't know how to do any of it?" he asked grabbing up the list. "It's not like I have brain surgery written down on here." He read down the list: *trim up the hedges, blow off the driveway, pressure wash the back porch* . . .

"I mean I don't know how to do any of it," she shot back reaching out for the list.

"You mean you have never done any of this before? Who did all the work around here before I got here?" His tone was kind of harsh and it was obvious that he didn't understand how someone just didn't know how to work.

"I don't know, I guess Dad did it all, I never really thought about it." She looked up at Jackson and his expression read of disapproval, and she didn't know how to react.

"Well I just don't know how you get through eighteen years and don't learn how to do work around the house." He tucked the list into the front shirt pocket of the mechanic style shirt that he was wearing and began to walk out of the garage and out towards the yard.

"Well you could teach me," she said in an almost whispered voice. "Would it be that hard to teach me?"

When he heard her say it, he immediately felt bad for getting short with her and he stopped in his tracks. He turned to her slowly to see her sitting against the bumper of the car looking hurt by his reaction.

"Of course I can teach you. Heck, if I can do this stuff anybody can." He walked back over to her and grabbed her by the hand and pulled her up from the bumper of the car. He kissed her softly on the cheek and they walked together out of the garage and into the front yard.

"Well, the first thing we are going to do is trim these hedges," he said taking a deep breath as if preparing to give a motivational speech. "It's not that hard, but it's real exciting," he added winking at her.

"Ok, trim the hedges, I can do that." As she said it, she bent over and picked up the hedge clippers that he had brought out earlier and laid on the ground. She walked over to the bushes with a handle of the clippers in each hand and froze. She stood there for a moment and then turned back to him. She had the same sheepish grin that she had had earlier. "Now what?"

He couldn't help but laugh at her. It wasn't a mean or judgmental laugh. He was laughing more at how cute she looked to him standing there in front of the bushes. He was doing his best to hide it.

"You laughing at me?"

"Oh no, ma'am, I would never. I was laughing at the bushes. They are funny looking bushes," he added grinning.

"Funny looking bushes, huh? Why don't you come say that over here, big boy?" When she said it, she took a snip towards him a couple of times with the clippers. "I'll make you shorter."

"Oh, don't do that. I just bought a new hat and it would never fit right."

"Well than you just watch yourself buddy."

"Ok, ok, I gotcha," he shot back with his hands up in the air as if he was offering them up in some type of surrender. "All you want to do is trim back the big stuff to kind of shape these things up a little bit. It's not that hard. The trick is just trying to make them all look even. I think you can handle it."

"Yeah, I can do it."

She made a couple of tentative snips at the bushes as if she was afraid that they might jump up and bite her.

"Come on, girl, just jump in there and cut 'em up. You scared of those bushes?"

When he said it, she got a look of determination across her face as she turned back to her project. She moved quickly into the first bush. Each one of her cuts was precise and each move was quick. He stood back for a moment and watched her as she started to move into a rhythm with the work she had started. The sun was moving up to the middle of the sky and the heat was relentless, but she didn't slow her pace. She would stop only briefly from time to time to receive a nod of approval for her work and then she would go right back to the task at hand. Sweat was beginning to bead up on her forehead, and he could tell the sun was getting to her after only about a half hour or so of working. Despite the heat she did not quit. Finishing one bush she would move quickly to the next and he would move in behind her to clean up all of the clippings.

"Well, that should do it," she said stepping back away after the last bush was done.

"Yeah girl, that looks good. I think it looks really good."

She did not even try to hide her satisfaction as she walked by him and casually handed him the clippers. "All in a days work, my boy, all in a days work. If you want me to I can teach you how to do that sometime." When she said it, she laughed to herself as she headed towards the garage.

"I am creating a monster," he whispered to himself with a smile.

"What did you say," she shot back.

"Oh, I said those bushes were a real monster."

"Yeah, you watch it pal. I think I have the hang of those clippers now so you better watch the trash talking."

He smiled to himself and then followed her back around into the garage. They went into the house to fix a glass of water, and it wasn't long before they were back out working on the next job. For the rest of the day they worked together side by side. It wasn't like it had been before. She no longer sat and watched while he worked. He taught her how to use the pressure washer, and how to check the oil level in the car. He showed her how to start the blower, and showed her the difference between one screwdriver and the next.

They worked together all day before they had finally checked off all of the things on his list. The sun had move on around in the sky and the heat was finally starting to give, as the sun made its way down behind the trees.

"You do good work," he said patting her on the knee. They had both found a seat in a couple of old rocking chairs on the back porch.

"Well, I had a good teacher," she smiled back grabbing his hand. "Thanks for taking the time to show me some of that stuff today. I know you could have finished all of that stuff about twice as fast if I wouldn't have been in your way."

"Oh, it was no trouble. Besides, you make my day worth it."

Neither one of them spoke for a minute. This time it was not because of a loss of words. They both had all of the words they could think of, but none of them were needed. They just sat in the two rocking chairs with their hands locked with each other and smiled. For Kristen, it was the first time that she had ever truly felt the satisfying feeling of fatigue after a long hard day of work. For Jackson, it was a welcome change to the fatigue that had become almost second nature to him.

"If you ever want to know how to do something just ask," he said softly looking out at the lake.

"Ok, I will."

"I mean it. The more you know how to do the less disappointed you will be."

"What's that mean?" She said looking at him.

"Well, the more you know the less you have to count on other people to do it for you. The less you have to count on people the less you can be disappointed by them."

"Jackson, what a horrible way to think," she said turning to him. "People won't always let you down."

"They will soon enough. They always do."

"I won't let you down, Jack. I promise I won't."

He didn't know exactly why he believed her but he did. He knew as long as he had her he would never feel alone. The rocking chairs creaked and moaned as the two of them rocked back and forth hand in hand to watch the sun set together for the second time.

"Hey," Kristen said turning back to Jackson.

"What?"

"Do you have to be home right now? I mean, do you have time to go to town with me?"

Jackson turned back to look through the kitchen window at the clock that hung on the wall. "Well not really. I mean I have to go fix dinner for my brothers, but after that I could go somewhere. Plus, I am pretty sweaty and nasty from all the work you did today so I probably shouldn't go out in town like this."

"Oh, ok," she replied.

"Well how about this," he said looking back at her. "Why don't you go take a shower and I will head home and take care of my brothers. I will meet you downtown by the old train station at nine. How does that sound?"

"That sound's, Mr. Bryce, like we have a date."

FIFTEEN

At nine o'clock Kristen was standing at the corner of Main Street just by the old train station and she was doing her best to find Jackson. She had forgotten that being a Saturday night in the middle of the summer would mean that downtown Cartersville would be busy with activity. The summer evenings in the main part of town were filled with small country bands playing familiar songs. Children ran carefree around the small town square and would have foot races from the train station to underneath the bridge. Lawn chairs dotted all over the place and the people sitting in them were happily carrying on conversation and filling their faces with barbeque that was being sold from vendors all over the street.

On this particular night the town square was busy all the way from Moose's drug store to Ross's Diner, so Kristen was doing her best to scan the crowd for Jackson. She was wearing a light blue sundress that fit the curves of her figure perfectly and helped to make her look far older than she was. She wore her hair down and the wind did its part to keep it pulled back away from her face to reveal her beautiful eyes and the elegant lines of her neck. She was nervous about seeing Jackson away from the comfort of the lake house and she could feel her heart beating.

She had begun to get worried when she finally saw him. To her it seemed as if the crowd parted as he moved across the busy square to where she was. He was wearing a white button down shirt that was untucked with the sleeves rolled up a couple of turns. He had on his blue jeans and all too familiar boots and she was sure she had never seen anything so beautiful in all of her life. When he walked, each step he took was with a sense of confidence; no hint of arrogance. Even the loose fitting shirt that he had on couldn't hide the power of the young man and for a moment she was sure that she had forgotten to breath.

"You look great," he said as he made his way to her.

"Thank you. So do you," she said, feeling her cheeks turn red.

"So what did you have in mind tonight," he asked with his hands half stuck in his pockets. When he said it, he wasn't looking at her but was scanning the crowd of people and all of the activities that were going on around them.

"Well nothing in particular. To be honest I kind of forgot all of this was going on tonight. I was hoping maybe just to get some ice cream. My treat," she added looking at him.

He looked a little insulted when she said it. "I may not have much, Ms. Taylor, but I can buy an ice cream cone."

"I didn't mean anything by it, Jackson, I just meant since it was my idea I ought to have to pay for it. That is all I meant. Honest." When she said it, she put her hand on his arm and immediately he forgot that he had even gotten upset.

"Well let's find some ice cream then," he said smiling back.

They walked around the crowd of people for a little while until they found some ice cream. After getting their cones, they made their way through the crowd and over to one of the bands that had set up on the stage near the old station. The band was descent and the music was a sweet classic country sound, but the crowd of people that was standing around only half listened to the music. Jackson and Kristen came up beside an older couple that was seated in a pair of lawn chairs near the stage so that they could hear the music.

"What do you think about the music?" Kristen asked looking over at Jackson.

"It's ok. I could do it better," he added with a wink. He had not meant to say it loud and did not mean anything by it, but the old man next to him had heard the remark.

"So you think you can do it better, huh?" the old man asked from his seat in the chair.

The look on Kristen and Jackson's faces was one of shock.

"Oh no, sir, I didn't mean anything by it; I was just talking. I didn't mean anything by it."

The old man in the chair did not seem satisfied with the answer. "I am asking you, son, do you think you can do better? Cause if you think you can do better, feel free to jump on up there and play something."

"Sir, honestly, I didn't mean anything by it."

Kristen whispered into Jackson's ear, "Can you even play?"

"Well sure I can play but I didn't—" before he could finish he heard the old man next to him yelling at the guitar player on the stage.

"Will, hey Will, this kid here says he can play and sing better than you," the old man was yelling over the music to the lead guitarist and the entire crowd had turned to see what all the commotion was about.

"Is that right, kid? You think you can do it better?" the man from the stage said to Jackson.

Jackson's face was blood red and all he wanted to do was run and hide. Kristen reached over and grabbed his hand. She wasn't sure if he could play or sing or do any of those things but she felt horrible about the fuss that was being made. The crowd that just moments earlier had not been interested at all had begun to jeer and yell at Jackson. Their cries were telling him to either get on the stage and play or get away so the band could keep on playing. Jackson turned to her as if looking for an answer.

"If you can play than play, or if you can run than run, but either way you got to do something."

He gave her hand a squeeze and then moved sheepishly over to the stage and took the guitar from the outstretched arm of the lead singer. Almost falling on himself, Jackson stumbled his way up onto the stage and took a seat on a stool that was sitting out in the middle. Kristen watched as he fumbled with the guitar for a minute or two as the cheers from the crowd got a lot louder and a lot meaner. To Kristen he looked confused, as if he had never seen a guitar before and he dropped his pick twice.

Realizing that things were about to get ugly quickly Kristen ran over to the stage where he was seated.

"What's wrong?" she asked in a worried voice. "I thought you said you could play."

"I can play. I have just never done it in front of people before."

The yells from the crowd were getting louder and sweat was building up on his forehead. He looked like he was going to be sick, and he seemed to have made a couple hundred people very upset.

"Well don't play to them," she said looking only at him. "Just play for me."

When she said it a smile poured over his face and he drew the pick down across the strings in one long motion. The chord was beautiful and he kept his eyes locked only on hers. Leaning up to the microphone, he opened his mouth and to a crowd of two hundred people solid gold poured out. His voice was soft and pure and young and hopeful. The jeers and the yelling stopped immediately as Jackson began to play and sing in one of the most beautiful combinations that any of them had ever heard.

Kristen couldn't move. When he had opened his mouth, chills went down her spine and all she could do was watch him. She never took her eyes off of his. His hands moved effortlessly across the strings and his voice carried across every corner of the square. *What can't you do, Jackson Bryce?* She could only watch him in total amazement until he finished his song.

When he had finished playing every one stood silent for a moment and no one clapped. It was not that they didn't enjoy the song; it was just that they all knew that if they clapped it would be over and they weren't ready for it to be over. He took down the guitar, and as sheepishly as he had moved on to the stage, he moved off again. The crowd erupted into applause and his face turned redder than it had been before. Kristen clapped furiously for him, and as he stepped off of the stage. she jumped up and threw her arms around his neck.

"That was amazing," she said as she slid down from around his neck. "I mean it; that was amazing."

"Thanks, that was just a song my dad used to sing to me when I was little."

"Well I will tell you one thing, Jackson Bryce, you sure gave those people a show," she said, as she slipped her hand into his as they walked past a crowd of people that were all slapping him on the back and thanking him for his song.

"I wasn't playing for them," he said pulling her around to face him. "I was playing for you." When he said it he pulled her in close and gave her a long hard kiss. In the cool summer air, with the smell of barbeque and cotton candy in the air, Kristen was the happiest girl in the entire world.

"Is there anything in this world that you can't do?" she asked looking up into his eyes.

"Yeah, pay rent," he joked with a half smile. "Now come on, it's bout time you get home.

SIXTEEN

In to the hottest part of the summer the two of them were always together. Jackson would pull up to the house early in the morning and Kristen would be up waiting on him at the door. Ed would give Jackson his job for the day and he would be off. Kristen no longer tried to stay in the house waiting to bring him a glass of water. Wherever he was working, she was there with him. He was always quick to steal a kiss as he would move from one thing to another. She had tried to help several times but Jackson would always stop her, and would throw down a towel or a shirt so that she could sit on the grass or on the dock and talk to him. He liked her helping but he enjoyed her company much more. He lived for those conversations and the work seemed effortless as they talked. When lunch would come, she would disappear into the house and come skipping out a few minutes later with a picnic that she had put together. They ate breakfast together every morning, and she would make lunch for the both of them everyday. She had also noticed that Jackson had been staying later and later in the evening, and so on many nights they ate dinner together, too.

Ed had put Jackson back to work on the dock. The new boards that they had put down a month and a half earlier had fit perfectly but the same storm that had damaged the boards in the winter had left the railing at the top of the dock in a mess. Ed had left Jackson to replace all of the railing.

Jackson and Kristen walked down to the dock that morning and stood out on the edge looking out at the lake. The sun had not gotten up high yet, and the air was surprisingly cool. Standing side by side, he reached his hand over and placed it in hers. She did her best to wrap her small hand tightly around his large callused palm and she squeezed as if to let him know she was right there. The butterflies that he had felt the first time he met her were just as strong, but the feelings had evolved. He needed these moments with her. With each touch, or glance, or kiss that she stole from him, she left behind a feeling of warmth that he could not explain. The look of sadness that he had carried in his eyes for years was gone, and had been replaced with a comfort and a joy that he didn't think he would ever know. With his hand locked tightly around hers, he pulled her in close to him. She placed her other hand on his chest and slid up on the tips of her toes to give him a kiss. Each time their lips met, he could feel the blood run up into his face, and his heart would pound furiously. When they kissed he never closed his eyes. It was as if he was afraid that this had all been make believe and he was scared to open them to find she wasn't there. Coming down from her toes, she smiled at him, and reached up to slide her fingers through his soft brown hair.

"I can't believe that you have been out here for two months already," she said.

"I know; I can't believe it has been that long already. Seems like I was walking out here for the first time yesterday."

"I guess the summer will be over soon," she said, with a look of sadness on her face. "I don't want the summer to be over."

"I know," he said, leaning down to give her another kiss, "But let's not think about that. Heck, you will probably be tired of me by then anyway," he added with a smile.

"Yeah probably," she smiled back, leaning in to kiss him again.

"Alright girl, that's enough of that. I have work to do."

She had noticed that any time she would bring up the fall, or school, or the summer being over, he would change the subject immediately. It was as if he was hiding from it. Hoping that somehow the summer would just go on forever.

"Well, get to work then. Quit standing around here wasting time," she said with a sarcastic tone. When she said it, she reached up to give him one more kiss.

"Ok girl, I mean it. Your dad is not going to think making out with his daughter is a good excuse for not getting this work done."

She laughed, "Yeah, I think your right. If he asked I would just tell him I came down here to see how the work was going and you were asleep on the dock."

"Oh yeah?" He said wrapping his arms around her in a giant bear hug. "You would sell me down the river like that, huh?"

"You better believe it," she said, struggling to talk under his squeezing embrace. "Now get to work," she said with a laugh.

"Ok boss, I'm on it."

He grabbed his hammer and crow bar and began ripping off the old railing that had been damaged around the dock. Kristen reached over to help him and he put his hand out to stop her.

"Now just go over there and sit down. I don't want you getting over here and getting in my way," he said with a smile.

"Who made you boss? I thought I was the boss around here. If I want to help I will help. You have had me sitting for a month. I want to do something. I know you're a big strong tough guy and all, but a little help might be nice, don't you think?"

"Fine, if you feel like working you can, but no breaks, and I don't want to hear you complaining that it's hot or you're tired or something."

"Hey, I can handle my self just fine, Mr. Bryce. Besides, if I get tired I will just go inside and take a nap," she added laughing.

"Ok," he laughed back. "Sounds like you are gonna be loads of help."

"Just hand me the hammer, tough guy, and let's get to work," she said tugging at her pants and bowing out her chest like he always did. He reached the hammer out to her and she grabbed one end in time to lean in to give him a kiss.

"Now you've got to cut that out. I can't get any work done if you are gonna be all touchy feely," he said.

"I will control myself. I promise," she said with a sheepish grin.

They worked together on the dock for the next couple of hours pulling off the old railing that wrapped itself all the way around the dock. The sun had finally poked through and the day had gotten hot quickly. They worked side by side and Jackson was enjoying every minute of it. He had conditioned himself for the heat over the last couple of months but he could tell that after a couple of hours that it had started to take its toll on her.

"Well, I guess it's about time for lunch," he said looking up at the sky.

"Its only eleven, Jackson," she said looking at her wristwatch. Her face was covered in sweat and she looked flushed from the heat.

"Yeah, but I am pretty hungry. Why don't you get some lunch together and I will finish up down here. I will come up there to eat if you feel like getting out of the sun."

Realizing that he was trying to give her a break, she paused. "Are you trying to get rid of me? I don't want you taking it easy on me."

He smiled knowing that he had been caught. "Baby girl, I am starving. You want me wasting away to nothin' out here?"

"Well, I guess I wouldn't want that. I'll go see what I can find for lunch. I'll be back in a minute. Don't you go doing all the work before I get back."

He laughed when she said it, "I promise I will try and leave some for you."

She leaned in and gave him a kiss. He could feel how hot her skin was against his, and the sweat on their arms made them seem to stick together. "I will be right back," she said as she turned to go back up.

He watched her walk back up the steps on the hill towards the house. He hated the moments in the day when he couldn't be next to her and he wondered how he was going to be able to say goodbye when the summer was over and it was time for her to go to school. The last two months had been the best of his life, and he wasn't ready to let it all go away when she headed to college. A couple of times over the last week he had come close to telling her that he loved her, but he almost felt the words were unfair. He knew he loved her, but he knew she needed to go and he didn't want his words to change her mind.

Waiting on his sandwich and working on the dock, he got lost in his thoughts. He knew that he would always remember every moment that he would spend with her. Each day when she would meet him at the door, and each night when she would lean in to kiss him goodbye. The moments didn't run together like so many others do. Every moment that he spent with her was fresh and different and he felt a new part of his soul come alive each time he was with her.

The day had gotten incredibly hot and his arms were starting to get tired as he finished pulling up the last of the railing. Reaching for the saw that he had brought down earlier that morning, he was preparing to cut some of the boards for the new rails when he heard her sing out to him.

"Lunch is served," she called as she made her way down to the dock. Her arms and legs were tan, and the pink tank top and short blue shorts that she had on showed off her figured as she bounced down onto the dock. "Got you some lunch, sir," she said in a sophisticated tone.

"Why thank you, my dear," he answered back. "You sure you want to eat down here? You don't want to go up by the house under some shade."

"Hey, what do you think I am, some kind of wimp," she shot back. "If you can make it all day out here than I can too."

"Oh, is that so?"

"Yeah, that's so. You may think your some kind of big tough guy, but I am just as tough as you are."

"Well, you're meaner if that's what you mean," he replied giving her a playful jab to the arm.

"See that didn't even hurt," she said laughing. "Now quit playing around and eat your sandwich. I have work for you to do."

Laughing at her tough guy act he said, "Just toss me the sandwich, baby girl, and I will go to work."

She smiled at him when he said it. She loved when he called her baby girl. She didn't know why. She wasn't big on nicknames or cutesy titles but she liked the way he looked at her when he said it. She felt so at home with him there on the dock. They both slipped off their shoes and Jackson rolled up his pants as they placed their feet in the cool lake water.

"A swim wouldn't be a bad idea," she said as her feet hit he water.

"Yeah, no kidding. It is getting hot out here."

"Oh the heat too much for you," she said, handing him his sandwich.

"Hey, I can take it if you can."

"Here brought you some water," she said handing him a bottle. "I promise it tastes better than the coffee." When she said it he couldn't hide his smile.

"Yeah, that was some pretty bad coffee."

"Well that's it, no more coffee for you then. You are permanently cut off from the coffee. I will never make you coffee ever again," she said in a playful but matter of fact tone.

"Promises, promises," he answered back.

They sat quietly for the next few minutes eating their sandwiches. From time to time they would take breaks from their sandwiches to splash each other with water. Kristen dreaded the idea of going to school. She had gotten so close to Jackson over the last couple of months and the idea of leaving him was more than she could bear. She knew it would never be like this again. She would be in school in the fall and he had just gotten a job in town that he would be starting in two weeks and would be working full time when school started. His old truck would never be able to last a drive all the way to Athens and her school work would keep her too busy to come home often.

The week before she had filled out an application to the community college that was there in town. She hadn't told anyone about it because she knew that no one would approve. She had thought that maybe she could go there for a while so that she might be able to stay closer to Jackson. She knew him well enough to know that she couldn't tell him what she had done, because he would want her to go to Georgia instead.

"It's hot out here," he said interrupting her thoughts.

"Too hot for you, huh? If you can't handle it just say so," she replied in a playful way.

"I didn't say it was too hot. Just that it was hot."

"I'm just saying if it is too hot for you there is no shame in calling it quits. You just go on back up to the house and I will finish up down here."

"Girl, you would cut your arm off with that saw."

"I guess it's better than cutting my leg off," she said poking at the scar on his knee where he had cut himself with the chainsaw a couple of months earlier.

"I am never gonna live that down, am I?"

"Not if I can help it," she said with a laugh.

Jackson took another bite of his sandwich and then wiped the sweat that had begun to bead up on his forehead. "It will be nice when the cooler weather gets here. Won't be so tough to work out here."

"Yeah, but by the time the cooler weather gets here it will be time for me to go to school," she said. When she said it, the mood went somber. There was only a couple of weeks left in the summer and it was beginning to become more and more real that it was all going to end one day.

"You will forget about me in a week once you get down there," he said looking out at the lake.

With a hurt look on her face, she turned to him. "I can't believe you would say that. How could I forget you?"

"Oh I don't know," he replied still looking out at the lake. He didn't want to see the look on her face. "I mean you are gonna be down there learning all these new things and meeting all these new people. Why would you want to remember this hick town or an old hick like me?"

"Because you are the best person I have ever known," she replied in a quiet voice.

"You must not know a lot of people," he replied turning to her.

The heat was climbing and they sat in silence looking at each other. The expression on her face was a mixture of hurt and worry. The thought of forgetting him made her sick to her stomach. She was sure that she would always remember these days.

"I mean it, Jackson," she said. Her tone was serious. "You are the best person I have ever known. You are sweet, and kind, and honest. You work harder than any person I have ever met. The way you look at me, the way you treat people. You take care of your brothers and you help out your mom. The only person that hasn't bought in to the fact that you are incredible is you. Once you realize it, there is no limit to what you can do."

The expression on his face looked stunned. "No one has ever said anything like that to me before," he said looking back out at the lake.

Her lip was starting to shake. "The way you hold me, and the way you kiss me," she paused. "I don't think I have ever felt so safe. You are the greatest man; you are the greatest person I have ever known." Tears started to well up in her eyes and she was choking back a flood of emotions. "The thought of waking up and knowing that you will not come walking down that driveway makes me . . ."

Before she could finish the emotion became too great and she began to cry there next to him on the dock. The tears were streaming down her face and she didn't try to stop them. Every time she thought about the summer being over she felt like she was going to burst. The tears had been building up inside of her for a couple of weeks and she let all of them out as she laid her head on his shoulder.

Jackson put his arm around her. He could feel her body quivering as she cried. He felt like crying, too. The thought of losing her was more than he could stand. Before he met her he had given up on life. It seemed sad that an eighteen-year-old had lost all hope, but in the last couple of months she had given it back to him. His life had changed forever because of her and he wanted so badly to find a way to keep her. Sitting there on the dock with her crying on his shoulder, he knew what he would have to do. He knew if he were to ever make a place for her he would have to find a place for himself. He didn't know what he was going to do, but the thought of losing her filled him with the strength he needed to go find it.

He reached down and lifted her head up off his shoulder with his strong but somehow gentle touch and pulled her eyes up to meet his. "Don't cry, baby girl. Pretty girls should always smile. It's the only thing guys like me have to look forward to." He reached up and wiped the tears off that were rolling down her cheeks. She smiled a half-hearted smile at him and sat herself back up straight on the dock.

She wiped the tears off from her face and looked out to the lake. "I miss you, Jack. I miss you already," she said taking a deep breath.

"I know. I know what you mean," he said reaching out to take her hand.

They sat there in silence for a minute or two. The moment was bittersweet and like all of the moments they had had they knew it had to end.

They sat with each other not saying a word taking comfort in having the other one next to them. Jackson squeezed his hand around hers, and he could feel her start to straighten back up, as she wiped her face off with her other hand.

"Well, are you just gonna sit here on the dock all day, or are you gonna get some work done," he said jokingly trying to ease the tension. He picked himself up off the floor.

She looked back up at him, "I am just the supervisor. You get back to work."

"Oh, is that right?" he said, butting his knee into her shoulder while he stood there over her.

"Yeah, that's right; now get back to work." When she said it, she started to pick herself up from the dock. Halfway on to her feet she reached out and placed her hands on his hips and gave him a shove. The push caught him off balance and with a scream he went toppling over into the lake.

She stood there on the dock looking down at Jackson's soaked head bobbing up and down in the water as if she had just won a game of king of the mountain.

"Oh very funny, very funny," he said splashing water up at her.

"Jackson, if you are not going to have any better balance than that—" she started in.

"Balance! I am pretty sure I was pushed. I was sucker punched. Now how am I supposed to get any work done in wet blue jeans?"

"Oh, don't be such a big baby. The sun will dry you out," she said laughing at him. "Now come on. Quit playing around we have work to do."

"Well at least give me a hand," he said reaching his arm out to her.

"Oh no. I am not falling for that trick. Your just gonna pull me in."

"I wouldn't do that. Now give me a hand. I have work to do." He had a serious tone in his voice and he stuck his hand out further to her.

"Ok. Don't you try anything funny," she replied wrapping her hand around his.

Before she could stop him, he gave one powerful pull, and she found herself being plunged into the lake next to him. When she brought her head up she wiped the water from her face and splashed at him.

"You said you wouldn't."

"You didn't let me finish," he said still bobbing up and down in the water. "I meant I wouldn't if you hadn't already pushed me in first." When he said it she flew after him pushing his head down under the water. They wrestled and pulled at each other. Each time one would come up to the surface the other would be waiting patiently to try and dunk them again.

Kristen reached out and put her hands on Jackson's head and pushed him deep under the water. She treaded water there in the same place for a second or two but didn't see him anywhere. She looked around the lake looking for him to surface. Instantly, she felt his hand wrap around her ankle but he came too fast and too strong for her to get a hand on the side of the dock where she was reaching. He pulled her under next to him, and they rolled around under the water until they both came rushing to the top for air. Out of breath and laughing, they both reached a hand up to grab onto the dock.

Water was dripping off of their faces, and they looked at each other still trying to catch their breath. Kristen's lip was trembling from the shock of the cold water and Jackson reached out with his other arm to pull her in close. She could feel his breath against her and it seemed to warm her up from the bottom of her soul.

"Jackson," she said pausing. "I . . . Jackson . . . I . . ." but before she could finish he brought his hand up to her face.

"I know. I know you do," he said with a smile.

When he said it he pulled her in close to him, and kissed her softly on the forehead first and then down her face to her lips. He wanted to tell her he loved her, but he knew it would make it so much harder to leave. He kissed her slow and long. He kissed her like it was the first time that it had ever been done, and chills rose up through his body.

"Well, we better find a way to get dried off," he said quietly to her. "I don't think anyone is going to buy the story that a wind blew through and knocked us both off the dock."

"Well you know how those winds can be," she said as she watched him pull himself up out of the water.

She reached her hand out to him.

"Now nothing funny," he said looking down at her.

"Don't worry, it takes a pretty rotten person to pull someone down into the lake who is just trying to help them," she said with a grin.

"It takes a much more rotten person to push somebody in in the first place," he grunted as he heaved her up out of the water.

Shaking some of the water off of herself, Kristen turned to him.

"Well I better go change clothes. Wouldn't want to work out here in wet clothes all day."

"Yeah, that would be horrible," he added, looking down at his soaking wet jeans.

She laughed, "Well, I will be back in a minute." When she said it she turned up towards the house. He watched her reach the top of the hill before he started looking around for the stuff he would need to get back to work. He pulled his wet shirt off and hung it on the steps to dry. As she ducked out of sight, he smiled to himself. He knew he would miss these days.

SEVENTEEN

The air felt cool as Kristen rocked back and forth in her chair. The sun had disappeared behind the trees and the darkness had spread all the way around the lake. She had still not heard from Jackson and her watch told her it was getting late. Her eyes were heavy and she fought desperately too keep them open. She brought her legs up and curled them up against her chest as her eyes began to drift off. She was fighting the sleep as she reached up and felt the necklace that she kept tucked underneath her shirt. She didn't know what was keeping him but she wished so badly that he would get there. The last couple of hours in the rocking chair had reminded her of thoughts, times and feelings that she had not dealt with for years. As her eyes fought their way closed, thoughts began to fade in and out. The last thoughts were of Jackson, and the day he said goodbye.

The day began as every day had since he had first taken Kristen into his arms. Jackson pulled up in front of the house early that morning and began his walk down the driveway. The new job that he had gotten in town would start in a couple of days and he knew that it would keep him too busy too come out to the lake house. Kristen was supposed to be leaving for school in a week, and even though the summer was drawing to a close, he had done a good job of pushing those thoughts out of his mind. He didn't want his last few days with her to be sad ones. He had made up his mind to go about it like nothing was about to change. It was the only way he could keep his emotions from taking him over. He knocked on the door, but didn't wait for anybody to answer before he turned the knob to go inside.

"Hey guys, It's just me," he called out as he walked in through the front door. Closing the door behind him he walked over into the kitchen to find it empty. It was strange not seeing anyone in the house. He had gotten used to Kristen meeting him at the door. He walked over to pour himself a cup of coffee from the pot that someone had made earlier. He only hoped that Kristen didn't have a hand in it. He opened up the door to the basement, and called down to stairs.

"Ed? Ms. Sandy, Kristen? Anybody down there?" He listened for a minute but didn't hear an answer. "Hello?"

It wasn't like them to all still be in bed, and he had noticed that all of the cars were still in the driveway. *Where in the world is everybody,* he thought to himself walking back around the kitchen and into the living room. He noticed that the door to the back porch was cracked open, and he walked over to see if they were somehow all out on the porch. Walking out onto the back porch he still had not seen anyone. As he turned around to go back into the house, he caught the faint sound of voices coming from the lake. Peering down through the trees he caught a flash of someone on the dock, and he sat down his cup of coffee and made his way down the porch and towards the steps leading down to the lake. As he got closer the voices got louder, and coming to the bottom of the hill he could see everyone out on the dock. Ed and Sandy were sitting in chairs out on the dock watching Alyson as she jumped out into the lake. Kristen was messing around on the boat, and she was the first person to spot him.

"Hey you," she called out to him. When she did everyone turned around to greet him with a smile. It felt so warm and he felt like he was coming home to his own family as he stepped out onto the dock.

"Well hey buddy," Ed called out standing from his chair. "Hoped you would find us down here." When he said it he reached his hand out to shake Jackson's and threw the other one around him in a quick hug.

"Hey Doc, what's going on," Jackson asked still looking a little surprised to see everyone out there.

"Well I told you when you first came out here that I was going to teach you to ski. We have two days left and I haven't gotten you out there one time. Besides, Kristen and Sandy told me I wasn't allowed to work you on your last two days before you start your new job."

Jackson laughed. "Well thank you ladies," he said with a smile beamed across his face. "I wish I would have known, Doc. I didn't bring any shorts. All I have is my work clothes," he said looking down at the jeans and black shirt that he was wearing.

"It's taken care of, buddy. I've got you a brand new pair of swim trunks sitting on the couch. Go put them on and get back down here."

"Wow thanks a lot. You didn't have to do that," Jackson replied.

"Oh yes he did," Sandy shouted out to them. "He has been working you to death all summer. It's a wonder you haven't collapsed. The least he could do is get you a pair of shorts so you could play for a couple of days." When she said it she cut a look at Ed, as if to tell him to be quiet.

Kristen called out, "Let's go now. Go get changed. We don't have all day."

Alyson was still swimming around in the water beside the dock with the floaties she had on her arms. She flopped around in the water and the floaties made her look like some kind of little buoy. She was normally the only quiet one in the group, but she called out to no one in particular. "Kristen loves Jackson, Kristen loves Jackson."

"Now hush, Alyson," Sandy said looking down at her daughter. Jackson's face was red, and he looked over to Kristen to see her looking down at the floor of the boat trying to hide her face.

"Kristen loves Jackson, Kristen loves Jackson."

"Shut up Alyson," Kristen yelled.

"Enough you two," Ed butted in. "Jackson, go get changed, buddy, and we will hit the lake. If we get on out there we can ski a little before the lake gets busy. I have a feeling you might spend more time in the water than on top of it. I don't want you getting run over by other boats."

Jackson was happy to turn and head back towards the house. Alyson's chant had embarrassed him.

"Be right back," he said, bounding up the stairs.

"Ok, the shorts are on the couch," Ed yelled to him as he made his way up the hill.

"Ok Doc, be right back."

Watching Jackson make it to the top of the hill, Ed turned to go back to his chair. He looked over at Kristen who was still getting the boat ready.

"Kristen loves Jackson, Kristen loves Jackson," he chanted in the same light tone that Alyson had had a couple of minutes earlier.

As soon as he said it, Alyson, who had managed to stay quiet for a minute or two, was back in to her chant as well.

"Now you two leave her alone," Sandy said with a smile. She looked at the expression on her daughter's face. She knew, as only a mother can, that Kristen really did love Jackson, and it made her sad to know that her daughter was about to have to leave her first love behind.

Kristen did her best to ignore all of them, and just kept her head down as she worked on straightening out the ski rope.

It didn't take Jackson long to change before he was back down at the dock. He was wearing the brand new blue and white swim trunks that Ed had gotten for him, and he had a smile that ran from ear to ear.

"How do they look?" he asked stepping out in front of everyone.

A series of over exaggerated "oh's" and "ah's" followed as he spun around like a runway model.

"Looks good, buddy," Ed said to him. "Now you look like you are ready to do some skiing."

They all climbed into the large ski boat and Ed fired it up. It was only a second or two before he had slammed down the throttle and the boat came lurching up out of the water. Jackson found a seat next to Kristen on the large bench style seat to the rear of the boat. Ed was driving and Sandy took the seat next to him holding Alyson in her lap. Jackson had only been on a boat a couple of times during the summer so it still gave him a rush when it took off. They left out and went around the bend of the lake and into a small cove. Ed brought the boat back down to idle and shut the engine off as Jackson stared nervously at him from his seat.

"Ok buddy, its time to get wet," Ed said to him when the cove had gotten quiet again. "Here is a lifejacket," he said handing him the vest. "It is probably going to be a little tight. We don't have anybody in this family with a chest as big as yours." When he said it, he caught a slap on the leg from his wife and a glare from Kristen as Jackson did his best to zip up the ski vest. The vest was tight and he struggled to get a deep breath as he moved over to the side of the boat.

"Ok buddy, I am going to help you get this ski on before you get in the water. I think it might be a little tough to slide on if you don't know what you're doing."

"Ok Doc, you know best. I have never done this before." He shot a nervous glance at Kristen and she tried to give him a look that said everything was ok.

Once he had his ski strapped on tight, he hopped out into the water. "Ok buddy, here's the rope," Ed called slinging him the handle. "Keep your knees bent and use your back foot like a ruder," Ed explained. "Don't be nervous. Just keep your back straight and hold on to the rope. When I take off try and lean back a little bit."

All of the instructions seemed like Greek to Jackson. He didn't understand what Ed meant by half of them and the water was giving him chills. It was still fairly early in the day and so the sun was not out in full effect. The combination of nerves and cold water gave him goosebumps all over his body, and his nerves were on edge.

Ed was shouting out more directions to him but he was in overload. He looked up at Kristen to see her smiling from ear to ear. She had a look like she knew what was about to happen and it was obviously funnier to her than it was to Jackson. Ed was still calling out instructions but the motor was back on and he could only nod his head back. Before Jackson was ready Ed slammed down the throttle and the boat lurched forward. Almost at once the rope straightened and so did Jackson's arms. His head never cleared the surface of the water, as the boat drug him for ten or fifteen feet. He finally realized that the best way to make it end was to let go, and when he did the boat sped off away from him making the lake seem very quiet for just a second.

The boat came back around to him and the roped slid past his face.

"Not bad buddy," Ed called out to him. "Just stay leaned back. Don't let it pull you forward. Try and keep your arms bent."

"Ok doc. Let's give it another try." When the boat turned around he caught a glimpse of Kristen and the smile that she had had earlier turned into a laugh.

The rope came around and all at once Ed threw down the throttle and they were off. Jackson managed to keep his ski under him for a second. It began to slice through the lake and his body began to rise up out of the water. He tried to make it the rest of the way, but the ski began to weave in the water, and he was instantly sent on a somersault across the lake. The first time had not hurt but the second one stung a bit as the rope came back around. Kristen was wiping tears off of her face as the boat looped back around to give him another grab at the rope. She was laughing so hard and so loud that it echoed in the small cove where they were trying to get a start.

Jackson was tired and his nerves were shot from trying to figure it all out with everyone watching. He did his best to get up, but after six or seven more attempts he had finally given up.

"Well buddy, it doesn't look like you are gonna be a pro skier," Ed said to him as he finally brought the boat over to pick him up.

"Yeah Doc, it is a lot harder than it looks. My old clumsy feet wouldn't stay in line," he said with a smile. He jumped into the boat squeezing his wet bathing suit all over Kristen's leg.

"Hey, cut it out," she yelled at him. "Don't be mad cause you can't ski." When she said it he reached down and grabbed her up in his giant bear hug.

"Not so tough no when I'm in the boat with you huh," he laughed squeezing her and swinging from side to side.

"Hey you two are gonna mess up if you don't quit it," Sandy called out. "You might get me wet. If you do I am throwing you both in."

When she said it they stopped their aggravating long enough to squeeze some water on her before sliding back into their seat.

Everyone else took turns skiing and Jackson enjoyed watching all of them do it. Even little Alyson did a good job and it was amazing to see her cut through the water on her tiny skis. The day felt perfect. The sun was up in the middle of the sky, but the breeze from the boat sliding across the water made everything feel right. He felt at home there with Kristen and her family, and the afternoon seemed to go on forever.

They had been on the boat for a long time and the moans from everyone on the boat meant that it was time for lunch. Ed wheeled the boat around and they sailed back across the lake towards the house. Jackson dipped his hand down into the water as the boat slipped through the lake. Kristen slid up close to him and he felt her slip her arm under his and wrap it back around. He glanced back at her and her face seemed to be glowing. The sunlight seemed to be coming from her cheeks and the wind whipped her hair behind her. He threw her a quick wink and then turned back out to see the shoreline zipping by them as the giant motor of the boat threw them across the lake.

After a couple minutes of riding Ed throttled down the boat and guided it perfectly back into place. As the boat neared the dock it seemed that everyone knew their job. Alyson tucked her feet up and slid out of the way. Sandy wound up the ski rope and tucked it neatly under the seat. Kristen reached out to the dock to steady the boat and quickly tied it off as Ed shut off the engine.

Ed turned back to his small crew on the boat. "Ok guys, who's ready for some lunch?" A resounding "Me" rang out and everyone jumped off to head towards the house. Ed reached over and patted Jackson on the back.

"Hey, maybe next time you will get it down," he said, even though they both believed there would probably never be a next time.

Ed grabbed Sandy's hand and helped her from the boat. He kept her hand in his as they walked back up towards the house. Alyson jumped off the boat and shot past everyone back up towards the house. Jackson moved slowly from the boat and looked back to see Kristen still sitting in her seat.

"Hey you two, lunch will be ready in a minute. I will call you when it's done," Sandy called out.

"Ok," Kristen and Jackson called out together.

"Well you coming?" Jackson asked holding his hand out for her to take.

"Thought you'd never ask," she smiled, taking his and to get out of the boat.

The rest of the family had made their way up to the house, and the lake had gotten suddenly quiet.

"You're not much of a skier, pal," she said to him stepping closer to put her arms around his waist.

"Yeah? I don't think your to hot with a pot of coffee," he said smiling. He pulled her in close to him and kissed her gently on the lips. "You look beautiful today, baby girl," he said pulling back to look at her.

"Oh this old thing," she said tugging at the wet t-shirt that hung over her bathing suit. "You don't look so bad yourself. I am a fan of your new swim trunks," she said tugging at the drawstring hanging from the front.

"Yeah and they were right in my price range too. Free," he said with a laugh.

"Yeah that suits me too," she laughed.

"Well I am starving," he said. Let's go get some lunch."

"Sounds like a plan. Lead the way," she answered back. She reached her hand out to take his and they walked with each other up towards the house. She loved him so much and she wished so badly that she could find the time and the place to tell him.

His heart ached as they made it to the top of the hill. He didn't want this summer to end, but the clock was ticking by quickly and his new job would start in a day.

Making it to the top of the hill, Kristen stopped abruptly at the foot of the stairs going up to the porch. "I need to get some clothes out of my car real quick."

"Ok," he answered. "I'll come help you."

They rounded the corner of the house to see her jeep sitting on the driveway. There was pollen all over it from the pine trees around the house, making the black jeep seem almost yellow. Kristen made it to the car and opened up the back door of the jeep. When she did a stack of papers came spilling out onto the driveway, and the lake wind whipped them around quickly. She scurried around to pick them up and Jackson moved to help her.

"See girl, I told you the other day you needed to clean this thing out. You know your car is dirty when trash is jumping out to attack you."

"Oh hush and just help me get these papers up," she said darting around the driveway to pick up the scatter.

Jackson had managed to pick up a handful of papers and he looked down to straighten up the stack as he walked back towards the jeep. The letter that he had in his hand caught his eye. On the top of the paper in bold letters it read Highland West Community College. His eyes scanned quickly down the page to see the first sentence that was written.

We are pleased to inform you of your acceptance. Classes will begin August 18 and registration for classes will be held August the 10th.

The look on his face was confused, and then immediately he knew what it was.

EIGHTEEN

"Kristen, what is this?" he asked handing her the paper.

A look of shock poured over her face. "I wanted to talk to you about this," she said. "I applied there a few weeks ago."

"Why," he asked. His look was stern.

"Well so I could stay here. So I could stay here close to you," she said.

"Kristen, what about the University? What about Georgia? You have gotten in. Why would you stay here?"

"I told you. So that I could stay close to you. I don't want to leave, Jackson. I don't want to leave you. I am not ready to leave you." She had a look of panic on her face and she moved closer to him. "Don't you want me to stay? Don't you want me to be here near you?"

"Kristen, you know I do, but you can't stay here because of me."

"Don't you think that is a decision I should make?" she said, raising her voice. "Don't I get a say?"

"Your parents would flip out," he shot back. "You can't pass this up."

Sandy stuck her head out of the front door of the house.

"Are you two coming in to lunch? I made some sandwiches. Come on, Jackson, you can't pass up a good lunch, now come on and get in here."

"Yes ma'am, be right there," he called back to her. He turned back to Kristen as Sandy ducked back into the house. "We will talk about this later." When he said it no emotion was in his face, and the change scared her. She had gotten used to his loving looks and the warmth of his touch. The serious look he used to have had been gone for a while and she didn't like to see it come back. He turned and walked quickly towards the house.

He wanted her to stay. He wanted her to stay so badly that he couldn't stand it, but he also loved her so much that he couldn't let her. He knew that there was nothing for her in this town and that if she was ever going to make something of herself she would have to go. It was at that time that he knew it was time for him to leave. If he stuck around she would stay too, and he would never forgive himself for it.

They walked back into the house and Jackson moved into the bathroom to change back into the clothes that he had been wearing. He walked back into the kitchen in his blue jeans and black shirt and slid into his seat at the table. Ed and Sandy chatted back and forth but Jackson just stared down at his plate. Kristen had taken the seat across from him and she was doing her best to catch his eye.

"Well lunch must be good," Sandy said, "cause you two aren't saying a word."

"Oh yes ma'am, it is very good; thank you very much," Jackson replied. He looked up at her for just a second and then fixed his eyes back on his plate. *She can't stay here. She has to go to college. She deserves that,* he thought to himself. He wanted so badly to take her up in his arms and never let go, and he could feel the tears welling up in his eyes as he thought about not seeing her. That summer had been the best summer of his life and he knew that it would be a long time before he would ever feel this way again. He finished the last bite of his sandwich and he pushed himself away from the table.

"Thank you, Ms. Sandy. Thank you for everything," he said.

"Well Jackson, it was just a sandwich," she said, not understanding the boy's tone.

"Thank you too, Ed. Thank you for everything." He stuck his hand out to Ed and gave him another firm shake.

"Hey no problem, buddy. I guess we will see you tomorrow then."

Jackson just nodded his head and moved towards the door. He moved to the door in the kitchen that led out into the garage. He never looked back at Kristen. He closed the door behind him and made it to the edge of the garage before he stopped. He put his hand to his chest and reached the other behind his neck, feeling underneath his shirt.

He was there for only another minute before he started up the driveway towards his truck. He heard the door open and shut behind him and he heard Kristen call out to him.

"Jackson, wait," she yelled with a tone of desperation. "Are you leaving already?"

"I have to go, Kristen."

"But I thought we were going to talk."

"Kristen, there is nothing to talk about. You have to go to school."

"Don't you think that's my choice?" she said, her eyes filling up with tears. "Don't I get a say? I am not ready to leave you, Jackson."

"I know I don't want to leave you either," he said, still back pedaling up the driveway. "But most of the time the right thing isn't the easy thing. You have to go. You have to go to school."

"Why are you leaving? You'll be here tomorrow, right? You are always here in the morning. You will be here tomorrow, right?"

she said again sounding more frantic. Tears were streaming down her face.

He didn't answer. He just stood there on the driveway looking at her as she stood there in front of the garage. He wanted to run back down the hill to her. He wanted to take her in his arms and not let her go, but he took one more step back towards the truck. "Don't cry, pretty girl. Pretty girls should always smile. It's the only thing guys like me have to look forward to." His voice was cracking and he could barely get the words out.

The tears were rolling down her face, and she stood there trying to call him back to the house.

"You will be here tomorrow, won't you? We can just talk about this in the morning."

"I have some things I need to take care of," he said. He made it to the top of the hill. "But I will be back when I get them done."

"What do you mean? You mean you have to run some errands? I can go with you. You mean you will be back tomorrow right?" Her legs and arms were shaking and she wanted to run but the flood of emotion seemed to paralyze her and her feet seemed pinned to the floor.

Jackson's face was wrecked with pain, and the tears were welling up in his eyes. He was trying to be strong, but his heart was slowly breaking.

"Jackson, I love you," she called to him from the other side of the driveway.

When she said it he froze. The tears came rolling down his face, and he hoped that she couldn't see. "I know you do. That's why I need to go." When he said it he turned to his truck. The tears running down his face were hot and his lip was quivering out of control. He fired up his truck and began to pull away. "I love you too," he whispered to himself as he pulled away from the house. He turned his rearview mirror down so that he would not be able to see her. After he made it around the corner, he pulled his truck to the side of the road and he cried until he had nothing left inside.

Kristen watched as he cranked up his truck and pulled slowly away from the house. She just knew he would be back tomorrow, and they would be able to talk about all of this. With the tears running down her face, she thought that she might even be able to convince him that it would be a good idea for her to stay in town to go to school.

When she turned back around towards the house she felt like she had been punched in the stomach. There, hanging from a nail at the edge of the garage, was Jackson's necklace. Reaching up to grab it she took it in her hands and fell to the ground. The emotion took over her body and she felt a pain greater than she had ever felt before. The tears poured fiercely down her cheeks and her hands shook as you sobbed over the necklace in her hand. She sat there on the driveway and cried for what felt like an hour before she had finally cried it all out. Her lip still quivering, she took the necklace that she had been squeezing in her hand and placed it around her neck. She knew as she felt the cold medal fall against her chest that he was gone.

NINETEEN

She hadn't heard the door open, but as she looked up from her seat there in the rocking chair she could see him standing in front of her. Her body felt like it had been ignited and her lip began to quiver as she looked at him. He hadn't changed a bit. He was just as she had remembered him. He was wearing a pair of blue jeans and a black shirt, and his hair was still cut short and neat like it had been. His arms and shoulders still seemed large set squarely on his broad chest. Her eyes traced up from his waist to his chest, and then to his mouth that was beaming with a smile that she had missed so much.

She stood slowly from the chair and she was looking at him squarely in his dark green eyes. He didn't move a muscle as they stood there looking at each other, and she could feel her legs shaking as she tried to steady herself. She couldn't believe that he had been gone for four years. Almost in an instant the time that had passed washed away and she felt like the same eighteen-year-old girl that had met him on this same porch years ago.

"Jackson?" she asked as if to make sure it was really him.

"Hey baby girl," he answered with a half smile.

Her lip began to shake and tears began to well up in her eyes. "I hoped you would come back. I knew you would come back," she said. Her voice was breaking and she was doing her best to keep from crying. She wanted to yell and cry, but she just stood there frozen in front of him. *Where have you been? Why did you leave me?* Questions poured into her mind but the words wouldn't come out.

He took a step closer to her, and she fell into his arms. She could feel his strength wrap around her like a blanket, and she buried her face into his chest and sobbed.

"Don't cry," he said pulling back from her.

"Jackson. Jackson, I missed you so much," she said between sobs.

"I missed you too," he said pulling her into him. She had missed his touch and she had missed the comfort that she felt when she was in his arms.

"I think you have something of mine," he said in a soft voice.

She ran her hand down to her chest and felt his necklace hanging there in its place. It had been there so long she almost hated to give it back.

"I do," she said, wiping the tears off of her face. She reached around her neck and pulled the necklace off. He took it in his hand and looked at it for a minute. He reached up slowly and slipped the chain over his head. The necklace fell down onto his chest, and she couldn't help but think that it looked at home.

"I thought you would never get here," she said still not able to get the words to come out.

He smiled at her, "It is good to see you. It has been too long."

She took his hand and pulled him to the stairs. "Come on; let's go down to the dock. I wanted to show you some stuff."

They walked down the steps slowly, and she could feel her senses starting to come back to her. Her legs were not stiff like she thought they might be from sitting in the rocking chair for so long.

"How is school?" he asked as they made their way down the hill towards the dock. Her hand was gripped tightly around his like she was afraid to let go.

"It's been good. I still have a year to go. I should have finished already but I changed my major a couple of times so it put me behind."

"That's ok," he answered still in a quiet almost whispered voice, "as long as you finish."

Having him there next to her felt incredible. She had not felt this way in a long time and her heart was beating faster and faster as they made their way to the dock. She wasn't nervous like she thought she might be. After feeling his arms wrap around her the nerves went away and the beating of her heart came from the excitement of having him so close. She wanted to ask him where he had been, and she wanted to know why it had been so long, but she didn't want to ruin the moment.

They stepped out onto the dock, and she could see the stars all over the sky. It seemed that there were even more out tonight than usual and the full moon that was out seemed brighter than it had ever been.

"I put those railings up myself," she said pointing at the upper level of the dock. "After you left I tried my hand at some carpentry work."

"It looks nice," he said, taking his hand from hers and moving over to look at her work.

"Don't put your hand on that one," she said. "That one is pretty loose. Of all of the railing that she had put up he had some-how managed to go to the one that she had put on wrong."

"You do good work, baby girl. I like it."

He wasn't talking much. He just moved around the dock look-ing at everything. She thought he looked as if he was reminding himself of where everything had been. He moved back over next to her and she could feel the strength in his arms as they wrapped around her shoulders.

"I missed you, Jackson," she said. Her lip started to quiver.

"Well you don't have to miss me anymore," he said. "I am right here."

A tear that had been forming in her eye fell out and rolled down her cheek. He reached up slowly and wiped it away.

"Why do you look so sad?" he asked staring into her eyes.

"Where have you been, Jackson? Why didn't you stay with me? I have needed you. I have needed you for a long time. Things would happen. Some good and some bad, and I wouldn't have anybody to tell. I was in love with you, Jackson. Heck, I am still in love with you, but more than that. The day you left I lost my best friend. I needed you." Her voice was getting louder and she was still fighting back all of the emotion. His expression didn't change. He just stood there while she talked listening to every word. She was glad that he hadn't tried to say anything. He just let her talk.

"For days after you left I would look out my window every morning to see if maybe your truck was in the driveway. When you never showed up it broke my heart. For months I would look at my phone to see if maybe you had called, and there was never a phone call. For the last few years I have checked my mailbox everyday, and there was never a letter from you. There was never a letter telling me that you would be back. There was never a letter saying, 'Sorry Kristen I never liked you that much anyway, but thanks for hanging out with me.' There was nothing. I didn't hear anything from you. When you left a part of me left to," she said as tears poured down her face. "A part of me left to. My heart, Jackson. You took my heart. I tried to get over you after a couple of years of not talking to you, but it never happened. Someone would say a joke, or make me laugh, or would put their hand on my shoulder and I would always look over wishing it was you."

He didn't move as she talked. The expression on his face made it seem as if he already knew everything that she was going to say. She felt like he was reading her mind, but she had been holding it all in for so long that she knew she had to get it out.

"Not a day has gone by that I haven't thought of you."

"I love you," he said cutting her off.

When he said it, she felt her knees go weak. She had wanted to hear him say it for so long. She had needed to know. She had always wondered if ever truly loved her, and after years of not hearing from him she had convinced herself that maybe he never did. She fell into his arms, and she felt the power in them as he wrapped them around her. She thought that she could still smell the sawdust and the sweat on his shirt that she used to smell when she would fold herself into his arms.

"I love you too," she said as he pulled her head up from his chest to look at her.

She leaned in slowly to him and when their lips touched her body felt alive for the first time in years. She left her eyes open when they kissed. She did not want to miss this moment. His eyes were shut tightly, and they held the kiss for what felt like forever.

"I was wondering when you were going to do that," she said smiling at him as they stepped back from each other. He smiled at her and they went over to the edge of the dock to sit down.

She rolled up the jeans that she was wearing and she put her feet down into the lake as she slid over to the edge of the dock. She looked over to see that he was already sitting there and had somehow already gotten off his shoes and had his feet in the water next to hers.

She looked at his leg just below the rolled up blue jeans. "You still have your cut," she said touching his knee. The cut looked fresh like he had just done it. The scar hadn't seemed to age, and neither had he.

"Yeah, still have my scar," he said looking down. "Do you remember that day when I came in the house?"

"Oh yeah, I remember. I guess it was the first time we had ever really been around each other. I mean other than that first day we met."

"Yeah. You sure did want to cut my pants all up," he smiled.

"Yeah, but you were too stubborn to let me," she replied grinning as she remembered that morning.

"You were glad when your mom sent you out of the room," he said, looking out at the lake.

"I sure was," she said back to him. "Wait, how did you know that?" she asked with a confused tone in her voice. "I never told you that." He didn't answer. He just smiled and kept looking out at the lake.

"How is your Dad?" he asked turning back to her.

"He is good. Same as always I guess. I think he is going to retire soon. You know him though; he will work until the day he dies."

"Yeah," Jackson smiled back.

"Your mom?"

"Oh Mom is great. She still asks about you from time to time. I think she really missed you, too, once you were gone. Well, I think we all did. You spent so much time out here it felt like a part of our family was missing."

Jackson smiled his large ear to ear smile when she said it. "I missed everyone too."

"Yeah, even little Alyson asks about you from time to time. I guess we all just missed having you around."

"I missed the free sandwiches," he said with a smile.

"Yeah I bet you did," she said. Looking out at the lake she asked, "Does everything still look the same to you?"

"Yeah, doesn't look like much has gotten done," he replied.

"Well after you left there wasn't anybody around to do any of the stuff you used to do. All of the projects and all of the chores just kind of went unfinished. I tried my hand at it but I guess I wasn't all that good."

"Well it's good to know I was missed," he said quietly. "So are you enjoying school?"

"Yeah, school is fine. I have met some pretty nice people, and the campus is pretty neat. I think I am ready to get out of there though. I am ready to go make some money," she added with a smile.

"So any idea what you are going to do yet?"

"Not really. I majored in biology so I was thinking about maybe going to Vet school. I don't know though. I guess I should think of something pretty quick."

"Well whatever you choose you will be great at it," he said. She smiled when he said it. He seemed to know exactly what she needed to hear. Her father would have launched into a speech about becoming this or that, but Jackson just smiled at her.

"Jackson," she said reaching over to take his hand.

"Yeah?"

"Where have you been? Why has it been so long?"

The mood was tense, and the only noise that was being made was the occasional chirp of the frogs that were moving around the lake.

He took a deep breath as if preparing for a long story, and then he began to talk. "I left because I needed to work, and you had to go to school." She already knew that but she didn't understand why he had been gone so long. He continued talking but his words came out in a blur to her. It was as if he was speaking another language, and she couldn't understand it. She tried to focus on his mouth, and she watched him form the words, but she didn't understand what he was talking about. She knew he had left to go to work, but she couldn't understand why and she couldn't understand why he had been gone so long.

He finished talking and he turned back to her as if expected her to understand. While she was trying to make sense of what he had said, he got up from his place on the lake, and he began walking back towards the other side of the dock.

"Where are you going?" she asked looking up at him.

"Just walking. Come on."

"Wait, what about your boots?" she said to him as she stood up.

"I will come get them later," he said.

He held his hand out to her and he waited until she had caught up with him. She wrapped her hand around his and they walked back up the hill. The conversation on the dock felt strange. She still was not sure why he had been away, but she didn't want to ask him again tonight for fear of upsetting him.

His touch felt incredible and she noticed that his arms still looked conditioned from the hard work, and she assumed that he must still be working pretty hard to be in such great shape still. Most of the guys she had known from high school had spent the following years drinking beer and getting fat. Jackson still looked lean and she could see the muscles in his arms flex as he swung his hand back and forth walking up the hill.

They walked around to the front of the house and to the pile of logs that Jackson had split and stacked years ago.

"I remember working on this," he said patting the stack of logs.

"You should; you were out here for a week or better," she replied. She turned to see two logs sitting out away from the stack. She smiled at him and walked over towards them. Still seeming to read her mind he walked over and stood the logs up on their end, and they took a seat on them facing each other.

"I used to watch you work from my window," she said looking up at her room.

"I know. I always knew when you were watching. I could feel your eyes on my back."

"I didn't mean to make it look all creepy. At least I wasn't standing in the window petting a cat or something like some creepy old women."

"I wish you wouldn't have seen me cry out here," he said looking down at the ground.

She had never said anything about that to anyone. *How did he know she saw him? He must have seen me move the curtains.* "Jackson everybody has a bad day. I never thought anything of it. You always seemed so strong to me. It was really the only time that I have ever seen you when you didn't look so strong. I wished that I could have come out here to you."

He didn't answer when she said he. He just looked down at the ground shuffling his bare feet through the dirt.

"You haven't changed a bit, Jackson," she said looking up at him. "I mean you don't look any older. You still look great."

"You are beautiful," he said looking up. "You always have been. I think you were always beautiful to me because you knew everything about me and you liked me anyway," he said with smile. "I always wanted to be a prince charming for you. I always wanted to be a knight in shining armor. I wish I could have been all of that for you."

"Jackson, you were. You are. You are still the best person I have ever known."

He stared at her and his gaze made her feel like he could see all the way into her soul. She didn't move as he seemed to study her all over.

"Of all the things I think about in a day, of all the places I go, and people I meet," he said in a quiet voice, "you are my favorite."

Her lip began to shake when he said it. She had needed to hear him say those things to her. She had needed to hear that he loved her. Everything he said was perfect. Just him being there made her feel better than she had felt in a long time. They sat there on the logs and talked for what felt like hours. She did most of the talking and he just sat there quietly listening to everything she had to say. When he would talk his words were soft, but they were perfect. As the night drug on she could feel her eyes getting more and more tired, and she let out a big yawn.

"You look tired" he said, standing from his log. "Come on."

He took her by the hand and they walked back around to the side of the house and up the stairs to the back porch. She turned to him and he put his arms around her.

She leaned up to him and gave him a kiss on the cheek. He turned his head and their lips met and she could feel electricity flowing through her body. His kiss felt perfect to her and his touch was amazing. They moved back over to the chair where she had been sitting, waiting on him to get there and she sat down in it as he crouched down beside her. She curled up sideways in the chair and he placed his hand on the chair and rocked it back and forth.

The gentle rocking of the chair relaxed her body and she saw him smile at her with his giant smile.

"I don't want you to leave," she whispered to him while he rocked the chair back and forth.

"I could never really leave you," he said leaning in to kiss her on the forehead. "I love you, Kristen. I will always love you."

She smiled when he said it. She loved the way the words sounded and she had waited for years to hear him say it.

"I love you too. I have always loved you."

The rocking of the chair and the comfort that she felt with him next to her made her eyes feel heavy. She was fighting off sleep, and she would open her eyes quickly to see him still crouched there beside her. She tried desperately to keep her eyes on him, and as she closed her eyes she thought she saw him scratching something onto the arm of the chair.

"Will you be here tomorrow?" she asked with her eyes closed. Her eyelids had gotten heavy and she couldn't keep them open anymore.

"I will always be here," she heard him say as she drifted off to sleep.

She knew she had dozed off, and so she smiled when she felt a hand on her shoulder gently rocking her awake. She was happy as she tried to open her eyes wanting to see Jackson there next to her. As the sleep started to wear off and her eyes opened up, she jumped back with a startled look on her face.

She jumped back to see her father kneeling beside her gently shaking her to wake her up.

"Daddy. What are you doing?" she asked, with a confused look on her face. Her eyes had not yet gotten adjusted.

He didn't say anything; he just kneeled there close to her and looked down at the ground.

"Daddy, what are you doing? Where is Jackson?"

Her dad still didn't answer; he just looked down at the ground taking a deep breath.

"Did you see Jackson?" she asked still with a confused look on her face. "He was just here. Did you see him? Has he already gone home? I knew I shouldn't have fallen asleep. He is probably mad cause I fell asleep. I should call him."

Her dad didn't move, for a second. He looked defeated as he knelt there beside her. She had never seen her father with a look like that on his face and it scared her.

"Daddy, answer me. Did you see Jackson? Did he go home?"

Ed looked up at her. His eyes were full of tears, and he didn't know what to say.

"Daddy, what is wrong? Why aren't you answering me?" She sat up from her chair and looked around, expecting to see Jackson somewhere on the porch.

"Kristen," he said as his voice began to crack. "There has been an accident."

TWENTY

Kristen stared at her father not understanding what he meant. She kept expecting for him to crack a smile and for Jackson to come walking out of the house.

"What do you mean there has been an accident?" she asked as her voice began to break and tears began to well up in her eyes. "What do you mean?"

"Tonight, there was an accident. With Jackson," he said. As a doctor he had had these conversations a thousand times with patients but as he looked at his daughter he fought to keep his composure.

"You mean after Jackson left?" she asked. Tears were streaming down her face and she didn't understand what he was saying.

The look on Ed's face told her he didn't understand. He didn't answer he just looked back down at the floor of the back porch.

"He was here," she said in a panicked voice. "He was here we just talked. See he came back and got his necklace," she said reaching down to her chest. When her hand made it down to her chest she began to sob without control. There underneath her shirt she could feel the round necklace still hanging where it had been hanging for four years. She choked back the tears. "He probably just put it back around my neck when I fell asleep. He was probably just going to come back and get it tomorrow," she cried. "He will just come back and get it tomorrow." A thought flashed into her mind. *His shoes.* "He left his boots on the dock. I bet he forgot his boots. They are still on the dock," she said standing up from the chair.

Her legs felt sore and stiff, but she shook them out quickly and ran down the porch and to the dock.

"Kristen!" her dad yelled as she ran down the hill towards the dock. She was crying harder now, but she was sure that she would find his shoes down at the dock. She ran from one end of the dock to the other, but his shoes were nowhere to be seen. She was out of breath and her head was spinning. He was just here. He had just been here. He probably just got his shoes when he left. She was confused and terrified. She looked up at the sky over the lake, and there was not a star to be seen. Heavy clouds hung over head and she looked furiously for the moon.

She went running back up the hill, past the back porch and around to the front of the house. Her tears were streaming down her face and she was trying her best to see in the dark as she rounded the corner. She made it around to the front of the house towards the stack of wood that had been sitting there for years.

When she got there she hit her knees and cried like she had never cried before. Just to the side of the pile were two big logs still laying on their side. The pain hit her like an earthquake and her body shook as she sat there on the ground.

She felt a hand on her shoulder and she turned to see her dad standing there behind her.

"He was here," she cried as her dad sat down and put his arms around her. "He was here. I talked to him. He told me he loved me."

"I know he loved you, Kristen, but Jackson was never here."

"Apparently he was driving over here, and he crossed over the line," Ed explained to her. His lip was shaking and he paused for a minute to collect himself. "He was driving too fast and by the time the paramedics got there he was . . ." but he couldn't finish.

Her dad reached up with a hand and wiped the tears away from his face.

They both sat there in the grass crying, both of them wishing that it was somehow a mistake. Ed stood up and he slid his arms around her, and he did his best not to cry as he carried his little girl into the house. He took her upstairs and placed her in the bed, and that night for the first time since he had left she cried herself to sleep.

The next morning she woke up and her eyes were swollen. She felt horrible, and she somehow wished that it was all just a bad dream. She pulled the covers over her head and tried to make sense of everything. Her body felt numb and the voices from downstairs seemed hundreds of miles away. She laid there with the covers pulled over her head for hours. Thinking that if she wished for it hard enough all of this would go away.

It was lunch time before she finally had the strength to get up and go downstairs. She was still wearing the clothes that she had worn the night before and she felt weak and her legs shook as she took the large spiral staircase down into the living room. She turned the corner to see her mom and dad sitting on the couch.

Her mom looked at Kristen, and immediately tears started to roll down her face. She looked away not trying to upset her daughter, but Kristen could feel the tears coming back up in her eyes too. It was real. She had hoped that somehow it had all been some sort of a mistake.

Her dad stood up as he saw her coming and went over to her. He wrapped his arms around her, and she began to cry all over again.

"It will be ok," he whispered to her.

"How?" she said. "How will it ever be ok?"

He didn't answer. He just squeezed her tighter and let her cry. Her mom moved over from the couch and she put her arms around them both.

The moment seemed surreal for all of them. Jackson had seemed like a son to them, and he had meant the world to Kristen. There were no words that could be said to make the pain any less and so they stood there together and cried, until the tears had all run out.

Kristen moved to the kitchen and got a glass of water. Her stomach was in knots and it was the only thing she thought she could get down. Sitting the glass back on the counter she passed by her parents and headed back towards the stairs.

"Kristen," her dad said in a hushed tone. "Here. This was in the car. It's for you." He reached into his back pocket and pulled out an envelope that looked wrinkled and mashed.

Her eyes began to fill back up with tears as she took the letter from her dad. She walked back up the stairs and into her room. Placing the letter on the nightstand she crawled back into bed and pulled the covers back over her face. She wanted to read the letter, but she knew that right now she didn't have the strength.

She stayed in the bed the rest of the day. Her mom came by to check on her a couple of times, bringing her water or Kleenex each time she came in. She would sit on the edge of the bed trying to think of something to say but the words wouldn't come out. Sandy didn't know what to do to make it any better and each time she would start to speak she could feel the tears in her eyes and her voice start to crack and she would walk back out of the room. It was late in the evening and her mom had stopped by to check on her one last time before she went to bed. She never said a word she just hugged her daughter and walked towards the door. When she had made it to the door she turned back around.

"I know he is gone baby, and nothing can fix that," she said trying with all of her strength not to cry. "But you gave each other something that no one can ever take away." The tears were running down her face.

Kristen starred at her mother with a blank expression.

"He gave you the greatest thing he could give you. Love. The best kind. The unconditional kind." She coughed and the words came out broken. "And you gave him the greatest thing that that boy could ever know." She paused unable to finish.

"What mom? What did I ever give him?"

"Hope, baby. You gave him hope." Her mother turned and walked slowly out of the room while Kristen turned back over to hide her face and cry.

Kristen rolled back and forth all that night. Falling asleep only to wake up again to realize that he was gone. She turned to the nightstand to see the letter with the large K printed on the front.

The next morning she got up and found her way into the shower. The hot shower seemed to clear her head a little, as she climbed out to dry off. She moved over in front of the mirror to brush her teeth and she did her best to fight back the emotions when she saw the necklace hanging in its place. Wrapping her hand around the necklace she whispered to herself, "I will get you back to where you belong one day, but you're just going to have to hang out with me for a little while longer." When she said it she could feel her stomach start to knot up, but she fought it back and finished getting dressed. Moving over to her room she put on some shorts and a t-shirt and started to go down to the kitchen. As she reached the door she caught the letter out of the corner of her eye that was still sitting on its place on the nightstand. She crossed over her room and to the night stand. She stood there over it looking down at the letter for a moment before reaching down slowly and taking it in her hand.

She walked downstairs and out of the kitchen, sliding the letter in her back pocket. She didn't see anyone around and after grabbing something to eat, she walked out onto the back porch. Her body still felt numb and she was doing her best to put one foot in front of the other. Each movement she made seemed sluggish and even the food she had just eaten seemed to have no taste at all.

It was unnaturally cool and even though the sun was out a breeze seemed to be whirling all around the house. It felt more like fall outside than summer. The air was crisp and clear, and not at all thick like it normally was this time of year.

She saw the rocking chair that she had been sitting in the night before. When she looked at it a lump came up into her throat. She walked slowly over to it pulling the letter from out of the pocket of her shorts. She sat down slowly in the chair. She looked at the letter for a minute or two as she rocked back and forth. The chair somehow reminded her of Jackson and the arms and large sturdy back seemed to surround her like he did.

She slowly opened the envelope and unfolded the letter that he had written to her just a couple of days before. She wanted to cry as she held it in her hands but she was all cried out. The handwriting on the letter was neat and small. Each word looked as if it had been carefully crafted on the page and the small block letters looked out of place next to the large script style K emblazoned on the front of the envelope.

Kristen,

Hey baby girl. I guess you're surprised to be hearing from me.
I hope you don't think that writing this letter is silly but I knew
once I saw you I would never get the words to come out right.
It has been a long time since I saw you last, but I promise you
that not a day has gone by when I haven't thought of you. The
day I left a piece of me died, and I knew that I would never be
whole again until I made it back to you. I guess you know that
my life was never easy. I didn't always get the breaks and most
days I had to work long and hard just to break even. I think my
life would have always been that way if it wasn't for you.

I know that no matter what happens in my life I will
always think of the time we had together and smile. You gave
me hope when I didn't have any and you gave me a reason to
laugh when I didn't have anything to smile about. I know I
am not a great man, but the way that you looked at me always
made me feel like I could be.

The day that I found the letter from the community college
that had fallen out of your car I knew I had to go. You are so
smart and so talented and so beautiful, and I didn't think it was
right to hide you from the world and keep you here to myself. I
left that day and moved up to North Carolina out on the coast.
You would be surprised how much people will pay a man for
some dock repair. I made a pretty good living, and I worked
hard at it. I was up there for about a year before I had enough
money to start hiring some crews and getting more work. I want
you to know that every day of my life from the day I left until
now has been for you.

I think I wrote you a letter every night that I was gone,
but I could never send them. I would look at the words there on
the page, and I knew you deserved more than that. No matter
how sweet the words were I couldn't make them strong enough

to reach up and hold you or warm enough to hide you from the cold. I wish I could have found the words to let you know what you mean to me.

I just bought a house back here in town and I think it's time I came back home. I have lived a lot of places, and I have been down some rough roads, but when I would think of you it gave me the strength I needed to keep going. You see, you are what home feels like to me. I don't know if I will ever deserve you, but I thank God for you. I hope you can understand why I had to leave, and I want you to know that I will never leave you again.

I guess you still have my necklace. I hope that in some way it always helped you remember me. On evenings when I would miss you so much that my heart would ache, I would walk out towards the ocean and watch the sun set. I guess in some silly way I thought you might be looking at it too and for a minute I didn't feel so far away. The only thing I regret about that summer was that I never told you how much I love you. I love you, Kristen. I love you with all of my heart, and I will love you forever. Of all the things I think about, places I go, and people I meet, you are my favorite.

Yours forever,
-I

Kristen finished reading the letter and a smile came over her face. He had wanted to give her the world and all she ever wanted was him. Her lip was quivering and the few tears that she had left to cry came rolling down her face. She missed him now more than ever, but as she read the last line she remembered that he had said the same thing to her in her dream. She knew he had been there, and she knew that he always would be. She clutched her hand around the necklace and rocked back and forth in the chair. A tear crept up into the corner of her eye as she ran her hand down the arm of the chair. There where she had seen him crouched down next to her in her dream was a small J carved into the wood. *He was here.*

For years after that day she would hear whispers around that lake house that sounded like Jackson's voice. She would hear footsteps on the dock and look up to find no one there. Each time she would smile because she knew he was watching. When the wind would blow the chimes, or if she caught the smell of sawdust in the air, she could somehow feel him there too. Every now and then when she missed him more than anything she would find her way back out to the porch. Smiling as she rocked back and forth on those lonely nights, she knew she could always find the love of her life waiting for her there in the rocking chair.